Traci Douglass is a *USA TODAY* bestselling author of contemporary and paranormal romance. Her stories feature sizzling heroes full of dark humour, quick wit and major attitude, and heroines who are smart, tenacious, and always give as good as they get. She holds an MFA in Writing Popular Fiction from Seton Hill University, and she loves animals, chocolate, coffee, hot British actors and sarcasm—not necessarily in that order.

One Night with the Army Doc
is **Traci Douglass**'s debut title

Look out for more books from Traci Douglass
Coming soon

ONE NIGHT WITH THE ARMY DOC

TRACI DOUGLASS

MILLS & BOON

Published in Great Britain 2018
by Mills & Boon, an imprint of HarperCollins*Publishers*
1 London Bridge Street, London, SE1 9GF

ISBN: 978-0-263-93366-6

MIX
Paper from
responsible sources
FSC® C007454

This book is produced from independently certified FSC™ paper
to ensure responsible forest management.
For more information visit www.harpercollins.co.uk/green.

Printed and bound by
CPI Group (UK) Ltd, Croydon, CR0 4YY

To my precious Carma:

Thank you for watching out for me and this story from across the Rainbow Bridge.

Until we meet again, love and miss you puppers!

CHAPTER ONE

"UNITS RESPOND TO trauma rollover. Motor vehicle accident. Hickel Parkway near Raspberry Road. SUV flipped several times, currently on roof. Three passengers involved—man, woman and young child. Man self-extricated, according to police. Woman and child trapped inside. Fire Rescue responding with Jaws of Life. Over."

"Copy. Unit A18 en route."

Dr. Jake Ryder replaced the receiver on the dashboard two-way radio, feeling the familiar buzz of adrenaline that always followed a call to arms pumping through his blood.

"Ready for action, Doc?" EMT Zac Taylor asked from the driver's seat.

"Always." Since taking over the Emergency Medicine Department at Anchorage Mercy Jake didn't get to spend much time out in the field, so this was a special treat. "I'll get things ready in the back."

While Zac steered them toward the accident scene Jake unbuckled his seat belt and moved into the rear of the ambulance. He grabbed some extra rolls of gauze and shoved them in his bag, then double-checked the batteries in his flashlight. His chief of staff's words from earlier that day were still echoing in his head.

"I know how you feel about the media, but this is Bobby's best chance at recovery..."

His best friend Bobby had saved his life once. Now Jake would return the favor.

There were no other options.

Even if it meant the possibility of revisiting the dreaded invasion of his personal life that had followed his Distinguished Service Cross commendation. That debacle was one of the reasons why he kept to himself these days. Other than Bobby and Zac, and a few other staff at the hospital, he wasn't really close to anyone. His ex and those reporters had really done a number on Jake back then, and now he had some reality TV doc ready to barge in and take over Bobby's case.

Exactly what he didn't need.

They swerved to a stop as Jake tried to picture this media darling doctor who would be waiting for him when he got back to the hospital. He'd never heard of this wunderkind guaranteed to be Bobby's medical savior. All he knew was what his ER staff had mentioned—that this traveling physician was all about the new and experimental, mainly at the expense of old-fashioned caring and compassion.

Not good. Not good at all.

Zac parked the ambulance, then leaned around the partition separating the front cabin from the treatment area. "Looks like a real zoo at the crash scene, Doc. At least the cops have the perimeter blocked off."

"Great. Let's roll."

Jake zipped up his pack, then pushed out of the rig with the heavy duffle slung over one shoulder. Sirens wailed and red and blue emergency lights blazed from all directions. One of the police officers gave them a rundown while they weaved their way toward the overturned vehicle.

"What happened?" Jake asked.

"From what the father told me, it was a moose," the officer said. "Ran out into the road and the guy swerved. Those SUVs are top-heavy, so the whole thing rolled under the strain. I asked him how many times, but he couldn't remember."

"Wife and kid still inside the car?"

"Yep. Both awake and talking. We've got a couple of guys trying to keep them calm."

"Awesome."

Jake slipped around the end of a fire rescue truck parked

diagonally near the wreck, seeing the snowcapped peaks of the Chugach Mountains rising like sentinels in the distance.

"Any loss of consciousness with the father or the other victims?"

"He says no, but it's hard to tell."

The cop kept pace with Jake's longer strides.

"The kid keeps crying for his toy, poor guy. We've searched the area, but haven't found any stuffed sheep."

"Got it covered."

Jake patted the side pocket of his duffle. The thing in his bag wasn't a lamb, more like a cross between a giraffe and a dinosaur, but any port in a storm.

"Is that the dad?" Jake pointed toward a man huddled beneath a blanket despite the warm September night.

"Yep." The cop veered off toward the demolished car again. "I'll let you get to work."

"Thanks." Jake turned to Zac. "I'll check out the father while you assess the wreck."

"Sounds good."

Jake walked to the agitated male standing between a police officer and a firefighter. "Evening, sir. I'm Dr. Jake Ryder." He set his pack on the ground near his feet. "I hear you had a run-in with a moose tonight?"

The guy, who looked about forty, and pale as death, nodded. "We're here on vacation and were out sightseeing. Next thing I knew this huge animal ran out in the road and everything happened so fast and—"

Recognizing the lingering signs of shock, Jake cocked his head toward the fireman and together they helped maneuver the father until his weight rested against a nearby squad car.

"Sir, help's here, and we're going to take care of you."

"What about my wife and son? Are they going to be all right?"

"The crew's working to get them out now." He proceeded

to examine the man for any obvious injuries. "What's your name?"

"Mark. Mark Leonard."

"Okay, Mr. Leonard." Jake palpated the guy's head and neck before moving to his arms. "Tell me if anything hurts or doesn't feel right."

"I'm fine. I just want to see my family."

"Please let me finish this exam first." He crouched to check out the man's legs and discovered a nasty gash on Mr. Leonard's left calf. "Looks like you banged up your leg, Mark." He unzipped his bag and pulled out supplies. "I'm going to tape this up before we take you to the ER. Hold still. It might sting."

"Ow!"

The guy jerked away and Jake tightened his grip. The cut wasn't deep, but it was filled with gravel and debris from the accident. If not cleaned properly, it could cause a bad infection. Jake had seen more than enough of that on the battlefield.

The father scowled, a bit of his color returning. "What the hell was a moose doing around here in the autumn? Don't they only come out in winter?"

"Rutting season."

Jake shoved the soiled gauze pads into a portable hazmat container, then unwrapped several fresh ones to cover the laceration before twining a bandage around the man's leg. Not perfect, but it would hold him until the Anchorage Mercy ER could suture the wound closed properly.

Talk of mate-seeking moose only served to remind Jake of the sad state of his own relationship status—or lack thereof. He wasn't completely pathetic. He was a healthy, red-blooded male after all. But these days he only engaged with women who knew the score, women who never expected more than a few pleasant hours between the sheets.

The firefighter beside Jake cleared his throat and brought him back to the present. He secured the end of the bandage around Mr. Leonard's leg with a metal clip, then straightened.

"Are we done?" Mr. Leonard tossed the blanket aside and tentatively put some weight on his injured limb. "Can I see my wife now? What about my son?"

"Stay here with the officers while I check in with the crew. Once they give me the okay, you can see them. All right, Mark?"

"Okay." The man's tense shoulders relaxed a tad. "Thanks for helping."

"That's my job." Jake packed up his gear again before joining Zac near the vehicle. "Dad's doing fine. What's happening here?"

"Mom says her arm hurts, and the boy is really frightened, but neither seem to have any serious issues. Remarkable, considering the shape of this SUV."

Jake stepped back and took his first real look at the damage. Shards of shattered glass littered the roadway and the sharp smell of gasoline and burning oil stung his nose. The whole right half of the car closest to him was dented and twisted, making the doors impossible to open.

A small voice called from the busted-out rear window. "Where's Lamby? I want Lamby."

The little boy's plaintive tone pummeled Jake's heart and took him right back to his last day in the Kandahar desert: to the acrid stench of diesel and melting rubber clogging his throat and choking his lungs, to Bobby pulling him from the blazing village amidst a hail of gunfire. Jake was supposed to have been the one doing the rescuing, but Bobby had done the saving that day.

They'd been best buds since their first day of basic training—a friendship that had only strengthened over the years. Bobby was his rock, his shield, same as Jake was for him. He couldn't lose his best friend. Not after everything they'd been through.

As the memories crashed in—of other emergencies in

far-off warzones—Jake slowly counted down in his head from ten to one, as his counselor had taught him, and the shadows gradually withdrew.

"You okay, man?" Zac thumped him on the shoulder, his expression concerned.

"I'm fine." Jake focused on the trapped family members. He'd always wanted kids of his own—always figured he'd get around to having them someday. Then time and circumstances and his career had slapped a quick kibosh on those dreams.

Jake battled the knot of regret tightening between his shoulder blades. Didn't matter. He was better off alone. Alone was safer. Alone was more comfortable. Alone didn't run off for a life in front of the cameras in glitzy, glamorous Manhattan.

He reached into his bag for the stuffed animal, then knelt beside the mangled car, clicked on his flashlight, and peered inside. Two huge dark eyes stared at him from the shadows. It was the child, still protected in his booster seat.

"Hey, buddy. My name's Jake. What's yours?"

The boy's bottom lip quivered and tears welled anew.

Jake hung his head. Here he was—a former special operations combat medic, trained to think on his feet with a hundred snipers poised to take him out at any second—yet all he wanted was to make this scared little boy smile again.

"Lamby's busy, but he sent a friend to keep you company. Want to meet him?"

"My son's name is Noah," the mother said from the front of the SUV, where she was secured partially upside down by her seatbelt. "He's four."

"Noah, my man." Jake held up the dino-giraffe. "This is Chewy. He'd like to come in and say hello…maybe sit with you until we get you and your mom out. Would that be okay?"

The little boy eyed him warily for several seconds before extending a tiny hand.

"Awesome." Jake passed him the stuffed animal, then turned his attention to the mother. "I'm Dr. Jake Ryder, ma'am. Are you doing all right?"

"My arm is killing me, and I've been pinned in this car for way longer than I ever wanted—but other than that, yeah. I'm fine, thanks."

The snark in her tone made him chuckle. "Do you recall what happened?"

"My husband swerved off the road to miss a moose, then glass shattered and flew everywhere and we were tumbling…over and over and over."

"Did you lose consciousness?"

"I don't think so."

"What about your son? Has he been awake the whole time?"

"Yes. I've been talking to Noah to make sure he stays calm."

"Excellent."

Jake shifted to survey the wreckage again. It looked like a bomb had gone off inside the car. He'd seen enough destroyed villages to know. Still, Jake and Bobby had been the lucky ones, coming home in one piece, without too many mental or physical scars from the war. Many others hadn't been so fortunate.

"Hey, Doc. Fire's ready with the Jaws of Life," Zac called from behind him.

"Ma'am, the crew's here to free you now." Jake started to retreat from the vehicle. "There'll be a lot of loud noise and some shaking, but I promise we'll have you both out soon."

"Thank you." The mom sniffled, her voice trembling. "Noah, sweetie? Remember the fireworks in July? All the loud booms?"

The boy nodded.

"It'll be noisy like that for a short while, but Mommy's right here with you, okay?"

"Okay." The little boy looked from his mom to Jake, the new toy clutched to his chest. "Bye, Jake."

"See you soon, buddy." Jake thumped his hand on the side of the car, then moved away as the firemen brought in the heavy equipment.

Moose!

Dr. Molly Flynn slammed on the brakes of her rented burgundy Range Rover and veered to the berm of this oddly deserted stretch of roadway. Well, deserted except for her and the behemoth creature standing twenty feet ahead. She shifted into "Park," then met the animal's startled gaze while fiddling with the onboard GPS once more.

Still nothing.

Molly shook her head and snorted.

"Go to Alaska," her executive producers had said last week. "A high-profile sports case is the best way to raise the ratings."

Normally she would've told them that her soon-to-expire contract clearly stipulated she got final say on all cases portrayed on her reality medical drama, Diagnosis Critical. But, considering she was on thin enough ice with the MedStar cable network, those ratings might be the only thing saving her career. And her career was all she had these days.

Besides, she'd earned this show, darn it. Built it from the ground up without any support from her father or her family. Now she'd do whatever was necessary to save it—even if it meant traveling to Anchorage, Alaska, a place that was a far cry from the hustle and bustle of Chicago.

She took a deep breath and stared at the lush forest around her. Maybe the middle of nowhere wasn't such a bad place to be after all. It might allow her a chance to escape the spotlight for a while.

Strange as it sounded, for a person who made her living in front of the camera, she'd always seen fame as a necessary evil. Curing the incurable, solving the unsolvable medical puzzles—that was her true love, the real driving force behind why she did what she did. In fact, the thought of being able to melt into the woodwork as she saved her latest patient sounded like pure bliss, if highly unlikely. Her network's syndication deals ensured that her show reached nearly every corner of the globe.

So much for privacy and anonymity.

Molly frowned at the digital clock on her dashboard. She'd been scheduled to meet with the chief of staff at Anchorage Mercy General Hospital twenty minutes ago, but her late-arriving flight, followed by the rental car's faulty GPS, seemed to have other ideas.

Add in the fact that the sun was setting over Cook Inlet, which was the opposite of where it had been when she'd left Ted Stevens International Airport at least an hour prior, gave her the sinking feeling she'd been driving in circles.

Overhead, an eagle swooped through the air, its low cries eerily haunting in the autumn evening. Despite her conundrum, Molly had to admit Alaska was lovely. Too bad she wouldn't have time to appreciate much of the gorgeous scenery, given her tight production schedule and the seriousness of her patient's case. Work came first, as always.

The male moose huffed and shook his mighty antlers before ambling into the forest on the opposite side of the four-lane road. Molly stared wistfully at the spot where he'd disappeared into the thick foliage, wishing she could find where she belonged so easily. Then her pragmatic instincts kicked back in and she focused on her current mission—find the hospital, locate her crew, save her patient.

Determined, Molly pulled back out onto the road and continued around a slight curve—only to slam on her brakes again. Now she could see why oncoming traffic had been virtually nonexistent. Judging by the array of emergency vehicles blocking all four lanes, there had been an accident.

As a licensed physician, it was her duty to assist when needed. Critics of her show always complained that she had the bedside manner of dry toast, but her real skill was as a diagnostician. And when she was working on a case everything else fell by the wayside—friends, family, romantic relationships. She'd sacrificed everything for her patients, and success was her reward.

A twinge of loneliness pinched her chest before she shoved it aside. The last thing Molly needed was a relationship. Especially since her last one had ended without warning. She parked on the berm, cut the engine, then blinked back the unexpected sting of tears as she walked around to the rear of the SUV.

Yes, maybe she did sometimes wish she had someone to share her life with. But, as her father had always said when she was a child, "Wishes are for fools. People like us seize what they want."

Trouble was, Molly had never felt like her father's kind of people. Or her mother's, for that matter. In fact there wasn't really a single member of her family, parents or sister, that she truly identified with. So she'd learned early on to live inside herself and bide her time. Now, though, it seemed she'd gotten so good at keeping her emotions bottled up she couldn't seem to show them at all—not even with the people she should. People like Brian.

She shook off thoughts of her ex and rummaged through the car for her emergency first aid kit. The pungent smell of spruce, mixed with a faint hint of fish and salt from the inlet, snapped her to attention.

Dressed comfortably for the nearly seven-hour flight from Chicago to Alaska, Molly didn't pay much attention to her appearance—jeans, sneakers and one of her favorite T-shirts that read, "Back Up. I'm going to try Science"—as she approached the nearby officer guarding the perimeter of the scene.

"Dr. Molly Flynn." She drew herself up to her full five-foot-four-inch height and held out her hand to the middle-aged guy. "Looks like there's an accident ahead. Do they require assistance?"

The cop looked her up and down, his expression dubious. "What are you, twelve?"

"Twenty-seven, actually, thanks for asking."

Molly adjusted her bag, undeterred. She'd put up with plenty of crap through the years because of her gifts. She'd graduated medical school at the ripe old age of twenty-four, with dual specialties in Immunology and Internal Medicine, but nothing made a girl feel less welcome and confident than having no friends and no one to sit with at the lunch table.

"Do I have to show my physician's license or are you going to point me toward the scene, Officer…?"

"Bentz." He sniffed and looked away. "The EMTs arrived a little while ago. Pretty sure they've got it under control."

"I see."

The man was dismissing her, but she was used to that too. Her mother had always been present, but aloof, and when her father had been home from performing amazing feats of surgical genius all over the world he'd only wanted to parade Molly around like some prize show pony instead of treating her like his beloved child.

"Molly, solve this impossible equation."

"Molly, impress my friends with another feat of mental acrobatics."

"Molly, earn my love by always doing what you're told, always being perfect, always performing, no matter what."

Her cell phone buzzed and Molly pulled it from her pocket, hoping for an update from her crew. Instead, all she found was the same dumb message that had been on her screen since before takeoff from O'Hare. The stupid text from her ex glowed brightly, its cheerful white background at direct odds with the dismal words.

I can't do this anymore.
Not sure you'll even notice I'm gone.

She resisted the urge to mic-drop the useless device into a nearby mud puddle and instead returned it to her pocket.

Looking back, she should've expected the break-up. Brian had always been complaining about her long hours and frequent trips, even though she'd been up-front with him about her demanding schedule from the beginning. And their blazing fights over the past few weeks had only served to resurrect painful memories of her father's indifference and cruelty when she'd been a child—the day he'd called her weak for crying over the death of her pet cat, the way he'd taunted her because she hadn't been able to make friends with the popular girls in her class, the night she'd graduated from medical school and overheard her father saying what a hopeless, awkward mess she was and how embarrassed he was to have her for a daughter because she'd been denied the membership of the Ivy League exclusive clubs and cliques her father had deemed necessary to mingle in his lofty social circles.

Even now those words gutted Molly to her core.

Brian, in the end, had pushed those same agonizing buttons, causing Molly to withdraw inside herself until they'd been basically nothing but glorified roommates. Still, she'd thought the year and a half they'd spent together rated more than a two-line text to end it all.

She guessed she'd been wrong about that too.

One more reason relationships were off her radar. Not even one-night stands. She preferred certainties to messy emotions, thank you very much. And, honestly, why bother when people left once you'd opened up and revealed your true, flawed self to them. Luckily, she wasn't likely to find a man who'd challenge those beliefs out here in Alaska.

Ignoring the lingering sadness in her chest, she concentrated on Officer Not Budging, still blocking her path. Intimidation was out of the question, given the guy had at least a hundred and fifty pounds on her, but maybe a healthy dose of mind-numbing logic would do the trick.

Whenever she felt overstressed or insecure, random facts always popped into Molly's head and out of her mouth. Blind dates, heated confrontations, heated situations of any sort, really. She'd ramble on and on about useless information until the poor victim's eyes glazed over and they wandered off in a fog of utter boredom.

Considering she was thousands of miles from home, hopelessly lost, and late for a potentially career-altering meeting, Molly couldn't get much more stressed. Plus, she'd done some light reading on the flight—facts and figures about Alaska, atlases, safety manuals, wildlife guides. Perfect for boring an unsuspecting cop to tears.

"Officer Bentz, did you know traffic fatalities in this state increased by twenty-six point eight percent from fifty-six in 2010 to seventy-two in 2011? Also, the percentage of statewide traffic fatalities related to alcohol-impaired driving decreased from thirty-four point three percent in 2009 to twenty-eight point six percent in 2010…"

Molly hid a smile. The man was fidgeting, his expression growing more uncomfortable the longer she droned. Soon the poor guy stifled a yawn and gazed skyward.

Chalk up another win for her near-eidetic memory.

"Most interesting of all…"

Officer Bentz looked at Molly again, his eyes as blank as his expression. "Go on ahead. I'm sure you can help with something. In fact, ask for Jake. He's with the ambulance crew tonight. He owes me one anyway."

"Thank you very much."

She turned on her heel and sidled through the maze of squad cars and fire trucks toward what she could now see was an overturned vehicle. During her emergency medicine rotation in Chicago, Molly had treated plenty of accident victims. That had been a while ago, however, and she'd been out of the ER trenches since signing on to do her TV show.

Fresh nerves and adrenaline quickened her steps and her pulse. Amidst the bright floodlights set up around the perimeter of the scene, Molly peered past the end of an ambulance in time to see a huge metal claw rip off a chunk of twisted debris from the SUV's side.

"Dammit." A man stalked over, his gray eyes sparkling with fury, his impressive build only adding to his imposing presence. "The cops are supposed to keep any rubberneckers away."

Molly looked around to see who he was scolding and realized, too late, that it was her.

"Get out." He stood at least a foot taller than her. And from the top of his dark brown hair to the tips of his black work boots the guy looked every inch the alpha protector. "Before you get hurt."

"I'm perfectly capable of taking care of myself."

She did her best to stand tall and forget about the fact this man was movie-star-handsome. Even with the beard. Molly had never gone for the lumberjack look before, but he made her seriously reconsider her life choices.

"The cop back there said I should ask for Jake."

His gaze narrowed. "Who told you that?"

"Officer Bentz." She pointed in the direction of her Range Rover. "I'm a doctor. Perhaps you've heard of me? I have a—"

"We're ready," said another guy. He was dressed in an EMT uniform, African American, maybe midthirties, and was calling from near the crash site. "Time to quit flirting and start working."

Her gaze darted from the wreck to the scowling hunk before her.

Flirting? With me?

If glares and glowers were this man's idea of how to attract women, it was entirely possible she'd finally met someone who was worse than her in social situations.

"Excuse me."

Molly started to move around him, only to be stopped by his hand on her arm. Never mind the warmth spreading through her bloodstream, or the zing of awareness crackling like fireworks. Verbal sparring was one thing. Unwanted contact was another.

Outrage stormed through her and Molly tried to shake off his grip. "Let go of me."

"You need to wait over there."

The first responder pointed toward the area beyond the yellow crime scene tape, his rigid posture and stern expression obviously meant to wither any defiance. He was a man who was used to being obeyed—that much was obvious.

Molly squared her shoulders and glared. "And you need to remove your hand before I remove it for you. Permanently."

The man's eyes widened slightly and a hint of admiration ghosted across his features. Before Molly could dwell on it longer, however, he released her, crossing his muscled arms across his broad chest.

"Fine. Stay at your own risk. I have work to do."

With that, the hunk jogged back to the wreck and joined the other man inside the half-crushed SUV. Soon they'd removed a small boy from the front passenger seat, stabilized his neck with a brace, then slid him onto a waiting body board before repeating the same with a woman.

Reluctantly, Molly's curiosity about the daring rescuer blossomed. She watched him cuddle the child, coaxing a smile from the little guy, and a fresh pang of loneliness stabbed her—along with a lingering worry about ever finding someone who'd look at her that way.

Considering her relationship with Brian was DOA, Molly had grave doubts. For a woman brilliant in her profession, when it came to her personal life she was one big mess. Not that flirting at an emergency scene was appropriate, but she wasn't good at it anyway. She'd always been a wallflower—one more check in her Don't-Date-Much column.

"Gurney coming through."

Molly barely had time to keep her toes from getting

crushed before the EMTs rolled past with the first victim. The two men hoisted the little boy up into the ambulance, then returned for the mother.

After they'd gotten the woman secured alongside her son, another man with a bandaged leg joined them in the back of the rig and the doors were closed. The hunk crouched near Molly's feet, gathering up scattered gear and shoving it into a medical bag. From her vantage point she couldn't help noticing how his tight navy blue T-shirt clung to his muscles and sinews and the way his black pants cupped his butt like a second skin.

Throat dry and head swirling, Molly panicked and said the first thing that popped into her mind—more random trivia. "Moose are herbivores and will casually devour seventy-three pounds of plant material a day in the summer. They like an assortment of shrubs, woody plants and aquatic vegetation; in the winter, their diet is more restricted."

She clamped her lips shut to prevent more useless facts from spilling out. Her father's voice echoed through her head, calling her pathetic. Worse, her last argument with Brian replayed in her mind like a bad song. The red flags were so easy to see now. She'd asked him to set a wedding date, to take their relationship to the next logical step, but he'd balked.

"Not everything's about logic. You solve everyone else's problems, but not your own."

The handsome first responder straightened and gave Molly a slow once-over. "Your facts are correct—except the bull that caused this accident wasn't looking for a meal. He was looking for a date."

Ah, right. She'd read about the mating season starting in late September in one of her pamphlets. Embarrassed heat prickled Molly's cheeks. Nervous, she smoothed a hand down her blond hair, still secured into two braids. Quickly she removed the bands at the ends of her plaits and ran her fingers through the stick-straight strands that wouldn't hold a curl to save their life.

The man's gaze followed the movement, the gray of his irises darkening to gunmetal. A throb of want started low in her belly, spreading like honey through her blood. It had been so long—too long—since a man had looked at her like that, and she found his arousal intoxicating.

"C'mon, Doc," the other medic said through the open door. "We got patients who need to be transported to Anchorage Mercy."

"Have a nice evening, ma'am," the hunk said, his stormy gaze flickering to her lips before returning to her eyes. "Be careful on the roads."

Molly stepped aside as the rescuer slung the medical kit over his shoulder, then climbed into the passenger side of the rig. The ambulance pulled away, maneuvering out of the tangle of vehicles blocking their path to the open roadway.

Hurrying back to the Range Rover, Molly started her engine, hoping to follow behind the emergency vehicle to her destination, all the while analyzing the new information she'd just gleaned. So he wasn't an EMT, he was a doctor. At Anchorage Mercy. Where they'd be working in close proximity.

Whoops. No.

Molly doused the sudden flare of excitement sweeping through her like wildfire. The last thing she needed was a rebound fling. Not with her career in the balance and her life in Chicago a shambles. Besides, she'd never chased after a man, never lived dangerously. At least not outside of the medical realm.

In the pursuit of a cure for her patients she'd tackle any challenge, take any risk.

In the pursuit of her own happiness? Not so much.

Still, one of the other reasons she'd chosen to do her TV show was to learn to listen to her gut. And right now her instincts were screaming that following that man and his ambulance represented her best shot at finding the hospital. So, Molly reasoned, this wasn't about a rebound relationship or a booty call with a hot doctor at all. It was about solving her next case and saving her show. She would worry about the rest later.

Squinting out the windshield through the gathering twilight, Molly realized she couldn't go through all the jumbled vehicles snarled in gridlock and still catch up to the ambulance, so she went around instead, driving her off-road-capable vehicle into the grassy gulley between lanes and past the still blocked section of roadway, then back onto the asphalt highway.

She might be late to her meeting, but if she was lucky she could still salvage this debacle.

CHAPTER TWO

"DR. FLYNN, I'M glad your producer was able to find a slot in the schedule for us."

The hospital's chief of staff grasped Molly's hand, his white hair and jolly blue eyes reminding her of Santa. He'd been kind enough not to mention she was an hour late. She was never late. Another lesson courtesy of her bully father. He'd always noticed any tardiness and the results had never been good.

"Your dad and I were classmates in medical school. How is he these days?"

Molly took the seat he offered. It seemed she hadn't quite outrun the looming shadow of her father after all. "He's currently in Beijing, conducting a training conference on the latest alternative techniques for closure of the open abdomen."

"Fascinating." The chief sat behind his desk and straightened his name plate. "Dr. David Carpenter" it proclaimed, in engraved gold letters. "And, please, call me Dr. Dave."

"Okay."

The cluttered room was the opposite of Molly's own pristine office back home. Amongst his papers and files were several family photos, in which everyone was laughing and cheerful. Smiles—genuine ones, anyway—were rare in the Flynn family.

"What can you tell me about my patient, Dr. Dave?"

"Yes, yes. Of course." He searched through a stack of charts on a shelf against the far wall then handed her one. "His name is Robert Templeton, though he prefers to be called Bobby. Thirty-one and a professional hockey player for our hometown team the Anchorage Anoraks."

"Anoraks?" Molly raised a brow. "Isn't that a type of jacket?"

Dr. Dave chuckled. "Yep. But it sounded cool so we went with it."

"I see. Says here he's an enforcer. What exactly does that mean?"

"It's not an official position on the hockey team, more of a tough guy. He starts fights to protect the smaller guys from taking the hits."

"Huh."

Molly had gone to a Blackhawks game in Chicago once, with Brian, and had had to cover her eyes during the worst of the brawls. Even a year spent in the ER hadn't prepared her for the copious amounts of gore and raw testosterone. If her new patient regularly partook in those kinds of brutal activities, it was no wonder he'd landed in the hospital.

"What are his current symptoms?"

"He was initially seen through our outpatient clinic for contact dermatitis."

She frowned. "How does a man go from a simple skin rash to cardiac arrest?"

"Good question." Dr. Dave sat back in his chair. "The treating physician gave him samples of diphenhydramine to take before he left and the wheezing started shortly afterward."

"He was allergic to the anti-allergy medicine?"

"It would appear so."

"Looks like they gave him point one cc of epinephrine to counteract his reaction to the antihistamine." She traced her finger down the chart documentation. "Could he have an underlying heart condition? A skin infection like cellulitis can cause a rapid pulse. Or perhaps inflamed blood vessels from vasculitis?"

"Nope. His CBC results were normal. No signs of an infection anywhere."

"Hmm." She flipped to the patient's labs, then went back

to the history and the physical. "No food allergies? He's not taking any meds on a regular basis?"

"None."

"And he's been complaining of strange scents?"

"Yes. Says he smells cinnamon and cloves all the time."

"All right." Difficult cases were Molly's bread and butter. She took them as a personal challenge. "Can you please order a CT of his chest to rule out Churg-Strauss Syndrome? His bloodwork may have been normal, but inflammation of the blood vessels in his heart, lungs and skin would explain all his symptoms. Also, let's start him on a high-dose steroid therapy."

"CSS doesn't have a good prognosis, does it?" Dr. Dave asked, his tone concerned.

"For patients diagnosed and treated quickly the life expectancy is five years. Untreated, Mr. Templeton would have a year at most. Of course there's always the chance this isn't autoimmune-related."

"You're the expert, Dr. Flynn. I'll get these orders to the staff right away." Dr. Dave smiled—the kind of fond grin she'd always wanted from her own father but never received. "You look so much like your dad."

Molly clasped her hands atop the file on her lap. Looks were about the only thing she and her father had in common. Always active, Roger Flynn expected everyone around him to adhere to his hectic schedule. To him, Molly had always been too quiet and boring, preferring to stay home and read a good book rather than operate in the jungle.

"Would you like to meet your patient now?" Dr. Dave stood and moved toward the door. "I believe your crew's waiting for us outside Bobby's room."

"Of course." She followed him out into the busy hallway. "And, please, call me Molly."

"Okay." He pushed the button for the elevator. "All the staff assigned to Bobby have signed the required releases except one. I'm still working on him."

"Unfortunately anyone who doesn't sign the forms can't participate in the care of the patient from this point forward. My crew films whenever I'm present, to make sure we get an accurate portrayal of the process." The elevator dinged and they boarded. "Perhaps this person can be reassigned?"

"Right." Dr. Dave chuckled. "And perhaps polar bears will learn to tap dance."

Molly glanced up, surprised by his sarcasm.

"This particular physician is a close friend of Bobby's and can be…stubborn when it comes to people he considers family. I talked to him again, before you got here, but he hasn't budged on the publicity releases. I'm afraid he prefers to keep a low profile. Dedicated workaholic, really."

"I see." Molly crossed her arms, wishing she'd had time to unpack her lab coat and cover up her casual travel clothes. "Well, I don't know anything about this Dr. Ryder, or his reasons for not signing, but those rules come directly from the network. Besides, treating a close friend or family member is a conflict of interest."

"Oh, I'm still the patient's official care provider."

The elevator arrived on the fourth floor and Dr. Dave held the doors, exiting after Molly.

"But Bobby signed consent forms allowing Jake full access to his medical records when he was admitted, and granted him power of attorney in case he's incapacitated."

Molly waited while Dr. Dave walked on ahead to the nurses' station, to speak with a curvy Latino woman whose name tag read "Gladys."

"Our boy available?" he asked.

"Yes, sir, Dr. Dave. He's got company, though."

"Dr. Ryder?"

"Yep."

"Great." He turned to Molly once more, his smile broad. "You'll like Dr. Ryder. He's a brilliant trauma surgeon, like your father. The youngest head of EM in Anchorage Mercy history. Cut his teeth on combat rescues in Afghanistan…"

Molly only half listened from that point, her mind still snagged on Dr. Dave's earlier words.

"He's a brilliant trauma surgeon, like your father."

Great. Just what she needed. Roger Flynn, Version Two.

"Hey, Mol. About time you got here," said her camera-man Rob, coming around the corner with her show's field producer, Neal. "Thought we'd have to send out a search party."

"Funny." She smoothed her hand down her shirt, then asked Neal, "Everything all set?"

"Everything except the guy sitting in the room with the patient."

"Molly?" Dr. Dave stood with his hand on the door. "Ready to go in?"

"Of course." She turned to her crew. "Give me a mo-ment."

Resolve steeled, she followed Dr. Dave into Bobby Tem-pleton's room. Whatever this Dr. Ryder's issue was with being on TV, she needed him to get over it or get out. Per-haps all those years of dealing with her father had made for good practice after all.

"Bobby, this is Dr. Molly Flynn, from Diagnosis Criti-cal. As we discussed, she'll be managing your case from this point forward." Dr. Dave placed a guiding hand on Molly's back and gave her a slight nudge. "Dr. Flynn, this is our local superstar—NWHL MVP Bobby Templeton."

"Hey." The burly guy gave her a small wave. "Honor to meet you. I watch your show all the time when I'm not training. My favorite episode was the one with the weird toe fungus." His gaze darted from her to the man at his bedside. "What's the matter, Jake? Tongue-tied around a beautiful woman?"

Dr. Dave smiled. "Dr. Flynn—this is Dr. Jake Ryder."

She turned, her polite smile freezing then falling. Dr. Ryder was the gorgeous rescuer from the accident scene. With her luck, she should've guessed.

He looked different now, dressed in scrubs instead of his navy and black EMT uniform. Not that the pale green material looked bad. Quite the contrary. With his stethoscope slung around his neck—no lab coat—he was transformed into a stoic professional, but she wasn't fooled. She'd seen glimpses of the passion lurking beneath his surface at the accident scene. In fact, just the thought of him rushing headlong into danger to save that little boy and his mother caused a fresh wave of giddiness to bubble through her.

But her attraction to him wasn't a good thing. It was a distraction she couldn't afford.

Molly swallowed hard against the lump in her throat caused by the tension between them. "Nice to meet you again."

"Again?" Dr. Dave asked with interest. "You two know each other?"

"I came across an emergency scene where Dr. Ryder was working on my way from the airport. He seemed quite… handy to have around." Molly rubbed her arm where Dr. Jake Ryder had grabbed her, her flesh still tingling from his touch.

"I should've guessed you were media."

The way he said the last word, like a curse, set her hackles rising. Common sense demanded she keep her head down, focus on work. Ignore this man who broke her concentration and keep her distance. Unfortunately he seemed to push all her buttons without even trying.

She met his sanctimonious stare directly. "What's wrong with the media?"

Instead of answering her question, the man looked back to Dr. Dave and exhaled sharply, his expression a mix of disgust and exhaustion. "Can we hurry this up, please? I'm coming off a thirty-six-hour rotation."

"Jake, please," Dr. Dave implored. "Dr. Flynn's one of the best in her field. You should reconsider signing those forms. Together, you two could make a fabulous team."

"No." He widened his stance, an immoveable wall of nope. "No releases. Not until I've seen for myself I can trust her."

It was the derision in his tone, Molly decided, that really got to her. She'd developed a thick skin over the years out of necessity, and could put aside almost any slight. Except one against her professional conduct.

Incensed, she stepped closer to the arrogant man, ignoring the heat of him penetrating her thin cotton T-shirt and the clean, soapy scent of his skin. Bad enough that she had to constantly prove herself to her father. She wasn't about to take the same crap from this pompous stranger—no matter how maddeningly attractive.

"My integrity isn't in question here, Dr. Ryder. Now, as per my network's guidelines, I must exclude you from Bobby's care unless you sign the required paperwork. I understand having the crew trailing your every step might be a headache, but—"

"You don't understand a damned thing, lady," he growled, his jaw set.

"Sorry, Dr. Flynn, but no one's touching me if Jake's out of the picture," Bobby added. "My prerogative."

Molly crossed her arms, all previous flutters of attraction for the handsome ER doc buried beneath a mountain of affront. She hated appearing so flustered, and cringed inwardly at the thought of how her father would judge her—letting her emotions get the better of her—but there was nothing to be done at this point.

"Then it appears we're at an impasse."

"Sure does."

Dr. Ryder mimicked her defiant posture and didn't give an inch. His gaze had gone positively flinty, and a small muscle ticked near his tense jaw, drawing her eyes to the hint of stubble shadowing his tanned skin.

"Why won't you sign the releases?" she demanded.

"Why do you think it's any of your business?"

His lips were pressed so tightly together Molly was surprised he could even get words out.

Dr. Dave coughed, the sound reverberating in the small room. "Jake, be reasonable. Dr. Flynn's a prodigy. She graduated high school at thirteen. In addition to her medical degree she's earned two PhDs."

He cocked an eyebrow. "In what?"

"Art history and genetics," Molly said, her tone equally frosty.

"Then I'll be sure to call you the next time I need to know the DNA sequence for a Jackson Pollack painting."

"Unfortunately for you, Mr. Pollack didn't leave behind any DNA samples for testing. Although it might be possible to extract a specimen from his exhumed corpse, given the lack of oxygen and sunlight to denigrate the samples. In fact, the oldest actual DNA specimens hail from Greenland, extracted from beneath a mile of ice…"

Molly's voice trailed off as she took in the dazed stares of the others in the room and her heart sank. Not again.

"Right." Dr. Dave passed Bobby's chart to her on his way to the door. "I've got other patients to attend this evening. Jake, you'll have to leave if you won't sign the releases. We discussed this."

"I don't want to be on camera." Dr. Ryder scrubbed a hand over his face.

"Why not?" Molly asked again. "Perhaps if you voiced your concerns—"

"He just doesn't, okay?" Bobby rose to the defense of his friend. "Can't Jake be an off-screen consultant or something?"

The door opened and Neal stuck his head inside. "We need to get a move on, Mol. The network's called me five times already, wondering when they're going to receive initial footage."

Molly hated to admit defeat, but things were getting desperate. If a compromise would get this guy to agree to the network's terms then it was worth it—at least for now.

"Fine, Dr. Ryder. But you'll have to work around my schedule. If I need access to Bobby you leave, no questions asked." Molly extended her hand. "Deal?"

He didn't move at first, and her hopes dwindled. Finally, Dr. Ryder grasped her hand, his voice sounding as reluctant as she felt. "Deal."

"Good."

Molly brushed aside the inconvenient flood of endorphins fizzing through her from his touch and handed him the patient's chart. She did her best work when she had colleagues with whom to brainstorm, and tonight she needed to bring her A game.

"Before the crew comes in, what's your assessment?"

Dr. Ryder thumbed through the pages, glancing at her with no small amount of suspicion. "Given the weird olfactory hallucinations, and the fact we've ruled out the other obvious choices, how about encephalitis?"

"The only elevated result on the CBC was a slightly higher than normal eosinophil level, which doesn't point to a brain infection."

Molly struggled to keep her voice steady. It wasn't the case that unsettled her. It was this man. He was too big, too masculine, too…everything.

Gladys came to check the patient's vitals. Molly wanted to question Dr. Ryder further, but his cell phone buzzed.

He pulled it from the front pocket of his scrubs, then scowled at the screen. "I need to get back to my department. Bobby, you're okay with all this?"

"Yep." The patient shifted on his bed, the plastic frame creaking under his muscled weight. "I'll call you if I need you, Jake. And don't hover. You just think you have to watch out for me because—"

"That's not why."

A look passed between the two men and the air in the room seemed to vibrate with a secret silent understanding.

Then Dr. Ryder headed for the door, calling to her over his shoulder. "May I speak to you outside, Dr. Flynn?"

Still trembling slightly from a jumble of unexpected confusing emotions, Molly took a deep breath and followed him out into the hall. She hated being this overwrought in front of people, especially her new patient, but this issue between her and Dr. Jake Ryder needed to end. She wouldn't let him destroy her best chance to save her show, even if it meant putting up with his irritating sexiness for the duration of her shoot.

"What are your next steps?" Jake asked once they'd reached a secluded corner of the hall.

The words had emerged more harshly than he'd intended, given Dr. Flynn's slight wince, but he couldn't seem to help it. Bad enough that she'd walked around that accident scene looking like some Disney princess come to life—all big blue eyes and lush blond hair—making him itch to hold and protect her. The tightness in his chest intensified, though his frustration was directed more toward himself than anyone else. Even worse that the first woman he'd felt attracted to since Kellie's departure was the media star Dr. Dave had invited to collaborate on Bobby's case.

Irony at its finest, folks.

Trust wasn't something Jake gave freely. He'd been burned too badly in the past. The truth was, he had a hard time believing in anyone these days, except his Army buddies and his tight-knit circle of friends. Intimacy required vulnerability, and Jake didn't do vulnerable anymore. Besides, he was a successful trauma surgeon. With his crazy schedules and on-call nightmares it was difficult to meet people, let alone have any kind of life outside his profession.

That was the excuse he was going with anyway.

And maybe Molly Flynn was the best at what she did—if

Dr. Dave was to be believed. That didn't excuse her impassioned speech about her sterling integrity—which, crazily enough, had only increased his foolish awareness of her as a woman. All he'd been able to concentrate on when she'd talked was her sparkling azure eyes and soft pink lips. God help him, he was in trouble here. Because she was Bobby's specialist and a TV sensation.

The last time he'd dealt with the press—after his commendation—he'd gotten way more than his fifteen minutes of fame. Worse, the glare of media attention had only intensified after his relationship with Kellie had fallen apart, with reporters poking and prodding into his wreck of a personal life like vultures at a roadside kill.

The last thing Jake wanted now was to delve into that shark-infested cesspool again, but he couldn't leave Bobby without an advisor in his corner. The guy had risked his own life to save Jake—literally. No way would he turn his back on him, no matter how uncomfortable the situation, and releases be damned.

During his time in Afghanistan he'd spent hours on the front lines, patching up men and women and ally civilians who'd given their all for their country. He'd enlisted initially for the experience, and to uphold the family legacy—his father had served as a Special Operations Pilot during Vietnam. But six years with the Seventy-Fifth Ranger Regiment had made his fellow soldiers Jake's surrogate family, his brothers and sisters. With them, he'd found a tribe of kindred spirits all addicted to danger and valor.

Day in and day out he'd vowed to protect every one of them with his life, if needed. The time had come to make good on his promise.

Rock—meet proverbial hard place.

"I've ordered a chest CT to rule out CSS," Dr. Flynn said, jarring Jake from his thoughts. "If you'll excuse me…"

"Wait." He pinched the bridge of his nose between his thumb and forefinger, doing his best to ignore the heat of her body wrapping around him, beckoning him closer. "I think we got started on the wrong foot."

"Yes, I think we did," Molly said, her gaze glittering with obvious irritation.

She wasn't going to make this easy. Then again, neither was he.

"Churg-Strauss Syndrome is a severe conclusion to jump to so quickly, isn't it?" he asked, puzzled.

Dr. Flynn sighed, the rise and fall of her chest causing the front of her T-shirt to hug her small curves. Not that he was looking. Nope. Definitely not looking.

"It's a remote possibility, yes, but it would explain all his symptoms. And I like to be thorough. Satisfied now, Dr. Ryder?"

Not by a long shot, sweetheart.

Sudden images of them tangled in his sheets, her long silky hair splayed around him, swamped Jake's exhausted mind. He backed away, alarmed. He'd just met her, for goodness' sake. Must be the lack of sleep. Had to be.

"Keep me posted on the results." Jake handed Bobby's file back to her, then headed for the elevators. "If you don't, I know where to find you."

The brief flare of awareness in her eyes made his own pulse kick higher. Apparently he wasn't the only one affected by this weird connection between them. Good thing she'd be on the first plane out of here as soon as Bobby had recovered.

All Jake wanted was an empty bed and peace and quiet. Unfortunately he still had about an hour of documentation to finish and a few patients either to admit or discharge before he was off duty for forty-eight blissful hours. Hours when he wouldn't have to see Dr. Flynn or deal with the odd blaze of emotions she stirred inside him, making him want to both kiss her and throttle her in equal measures.

It was crazy. And then there was that slight yearning that crept into her expression sometimes, like when they'd been standing in the hallway discussing the case—a hesitation that called to his inner protector. Dangerous, that, since it threatened those precious walls he'd built—the ones meant to keep his heart from getting torn out and stomped on again.

Honestly, it had been so long since he'd had a significant other he couldn't remember what it was like. During the last few months before Kellie had left him things had been so strained they'd just been going through the motions. Even so, the last thing he'd expected had been her accepting a network job in New York City without even discussing it with him. Blindsided didn't begin to cover how he'd felt at the time. How he still felt, in some ways.

Eighteen months had passed and it still hacked Jake off whenever he remembered. He'd thought they had something good together—something real, something lasting.

He guessed that just went to show what an idiot he was when it came to love.

Good thing he was brilliant in his career. Saving lives was what he did, who he was. Since his fiancée's abrupt departure Jake had thrown himself into saving his patients, into making their lives better. It helped him forget about the loneliness, the doubts. Doubts that if he hadn't been enough for Kellie, why should he believe he'd ever be enough for anyone else?

One more reason to stick with short-term flings.

No muss, no fuss, no commitment. No chance for heartbreak and disappointment.

Yeah, perhaps if circumstances had been different, and he and Molly had met at some bar on a lonely night, they might've shared more than a medical case. Jake might've let her get a glimpse of the man locked behind those staunch barriers…might've let that instant connection between them evolve into something more.

But not now. Now he'd consult on Bobby's case, be his advocate. That was all.

The elevator dinged and Jake climbed on board, ignoring the niggle of regret that bored into his chest.

Once he reached the first floor, he headed to his office near the ER and the inbox full of patient files awaiting his attention.

Yawning, he took a seat and grabbed the top chart, scanning the lab reports and papers inside before making his notations. Work kept him busy and sane. Work also kept him distracted. The constant hustle and bustle was part of the reason he spent so much time here. The other part was the fact that he didn't have much going on outside of this place.

Determined to stay on track, Jake worked his way through the stack of charts until they were finished, then grabbed his keys and did a final check on the condition of his patients at the nurses' station. Once that was taken care of for the night, Jake headed home.

He climbed behind the wheel of his truck and cranked the engine, squeezing his tired eyes shut. Bobby's words during that firefight in Kandahar were ringing in his head like a clarion call.

"We'll make it, bud…"

And they would No matter what trials and temptations Dr. Molly Flynn might pose.

CHAPTER THREE

"JUST PUT YOUR arm around it!" Rob yelled to Molly from behind a swath of thick rope. "Pretend it's that hot doc at the hospital."

She gave her cameraman a peeved stare. Had her attraction to Jake Ryder been that apparent? If Rob and Neal's smirks were any indication then, yes, it had. Ugh. She usually kept a tight lid on her emotions. One more casualty of her jet lag and post-break-up-from-Brian funk.

Fabulous.

Exhaling loudly, Molly did her best to snuggle up to the world's largest broccoli spear—weighing in at an astonishing thirty-nine pounds—and flashed a TV-perfect fake smile for the camera. The thing smelled like dirt and towered above her, its fanned floret casting ominous shadows. She'd read that Alaska was famous for its abnormally large produce, and here she was, within breathing distance of the proof.

"Perfect!" Rob gave her a thumbs-up while Neal texted on his phone.

Remarkably, they seemed to have good cell service out here—better than she'd had on her drive in from the airport the night before.

"I want to grab a corn dog before we head to the next location. Mol, you want anything?"

She shook her head. They'd set out this morning to capture some of the local flavor before her case took precedence. Bright and early, they'd packed up her Range Rover to explore all the area had to offer. After stopping at a diner for breakfast, and taking some exterior shots at the must-see spots in Anchorage—the modern curved sculptures outside the Z.J. Loussac Public Library, the gorgeous Native American exhibits at Rasmuson Center, the rustic quaintness of the Oscar Anderson House Museum, the city's oldest residence—they'd driven forty minutes north to the small town of Palmer and the Alaska State Fair.

She released the giant cruciferous vegetable and scanned the vendors there, selling everything from pretzels to enormous ice cream cones. The air smelled of sweet popped corn and deep-fried dough. Rob tottered off to get his corn dog and Neal linked arms with Molly, leading her down a path designated as "The Purple Trail" to buy something called a Doughnut Burger.

"C'mon. It's guaranteed to make you gain ten pounds." He gave her a wink and placed his order but she passed.

She tried to eat healthily, even while traveling. If she ever let herself go physically her father would be the first to comment, so it was safer to not go down that road to begin with—no matter how tempting at times like this.

After collecting his food, she and Neal took a seat at one of the many wooden picnic tables to wait for Rob. The two guys had been a couple since before she'd joined the network, though they kept their personal relationship out of the office.

"Are you sure you don't want a bite?" Neal asked.

Molly eyed the thick caribou steak patty between two slabs of grilled glazed doughnut, ketchup and mustard dripping down its sides, with trepidation. She could almost feel her arteries clogging. "Uh…no thanks."

"It's so scrumptious." Neal wiped his face with his napkin, speaking to her around a mouthful of food. "At least try a corn fritter with honey butter dipping sauce. They're delicious."

"I'm still stuffed from breakfast, really."

Molly pulled her phone from her pocket and zipped through her emails while Rob took a seat on the bench beside Neal and slid a plate in front of her.

"I got you a funnel cake, Mol. My treat." Rob grinned. "Extra powdered sugar."

Frowning, she stared down at the greasy confection. Its yeasty aroma was enticing, despite its odd look. She'd heard of these things, but never tried one herself. Tentatively she pulled off a tiny chunk and ate it. The treat melted in her mouth, releasing its sweet, rich goodness.

Eyes wide, Molly blinked at her smiling crew. "That's amazing."

"Told you." Neal winked, then nudged Rob with his elbow.

She gobbled down more of the sweet deliciousness before answering her buzzing phone without checking the caller ID, assuming it would be the hospital. "Dr. Molly Flynn."

"Hello, dear. Did you hear about Martha?"

"Yes, Mother."

Neal raised a speculative brow and Molly swiveled on her bench to face in the opposite direction. She and her older sister Martha weren't exactly close, but that hadn't kept Molly from escaping the dreaded Baby Aboard! email blitz.

"I heard."

"Then you'll help me plan the shower?"

"She's five months along." Molly squinted into the hazy morning sunshine.

"Never too early to plan, dear. Not if you want the best."

And of course Martha would have the best. She always got the best—from prom dresses to husbands.

"We need to reserve a room and order flowers. Pick a caterer and a cake maker too."

"It's a baby shower, Mother. Not a wedding."

A cute little girl dressed to perform in one of the fair's many shows waddled by and Molly smiled. She'd always loved children, but having her own someday seemed farther out of reach than ever. Mainly because of the belief her father had instilled within her every day of her childhood—that if people saw her true fallible self, her imperfections and quirks, they wouldn't love her, couldn't love her. So she hid behind her slick professionalism, her media persona, never letting anyone get too close to the truth.

"Speaking of weddings—how are things with Brian?" her mother asked.

The question hit Molly like a sucker punch. For a moment she considered lying about their separation, but her mother would find out soon enough—if she didn't already know. "We're taking a break."

"Break?"

"Yes." Molly reached behind her and grabbed the remaining huge chunk of funnel cake, shoving it in her mouth without thinking. "He's busy with stocks and bonds and I'm swamped with shooting in Anchorage for the next few weeks, so it's fine."

"I see." Her mother's tone suggested that she'd seen straight through Molly's crap. "You can't keep doing this, dear."

"Doing what?"

"Putting your personal life on hold. You're not getting any younger."

Exactly what she didn't need today. A baby pep-talk from her mother. When she was a teen, Molly had often wished she had the kind of parents that showed up in her favorite sitcoms. The loving, supportive variety, who never pushed their kids to do things they didn't want and loved them unconditionally for who they were. But real life wasn't like TV, and usually you just had to do the best with what you'd got.

Her shoulders slumped as the scent of fresh kettle corn drifted on the breeze. Molly's lifelong imposed restraint buckled under the pressure and she all but tripped over herself on her way to buy a bag. After all, she should experiment while she still had the chance, right?

Molly changed the subject while she waited in line. "What are my duties for the shower?"

"Decorations. And I'll see if your father knows anyone."

"For what?"

"For you. When will you be back home, dear?"

"I just got to Alaska."

Not to mention the fact the last thing she wanted was a blind date with one of her father's legion of devoted clones.

Molly paid and thanked the vendor then returned to the table with her popcorn. "I'm not ready to date anyone else yet. Besides, there's a colleague here who's giving me issues."

"Really? Is he attractive?"

"No."

Yes. All she had to do was picture Dr. Ryder's stormy gray eyes, his chiseled jaw and toned muscles, and molten heat spread outward from her core to sizzle through her bloodstream. It seemed the gorgeous man caused her problems even when he wasn't around.

If only he wasn't her new colleague.

If only…what?

No. That line of thinking was completely unacceptable. They were working together. Molly was only here temporarily. Dr. Ryder treated her as if she harbored a deadly contagious disease. It was all so irritating and annoying and incredibly intriguing.

Scowling, she shoved another handful of popcorn in her mouth. "What difference does it make? He's a nuisance. Challenging everything I do, every order I give."

"Perhaps if you tried charm instead of your usual abruptness you might get further."

Molly checked her watch. If they were going to fit another location in before she went to the hospital, they had to get a move on. "I need to go."

"Thank you for proving my point, dear."

She felt her mother's disapproval like a slap.

"I'll call you next week with a list of supplies."

"Fine," Molly said, though the line had already gone

dead. Talk about abrupt. Clicking off her phone, she turned back to her crew. "Have you guys decided on our last stop?"

"We have." Neal gave her his devious smile—the one that always warned of mischief ahead. "You ready?"

She tossed her trash in a nearby bin, then followed her crew toward the exit. "Can I at least get a clue where we're headed?"

"I talked to one of the ER nurses yesterday before you arrived," Rob said. "She's part of a volunteer mountain rescue group. They're practicing maneuvers today. Neal thinks it might be a nice way to segue into the local medical scene."

"Ready, Ryder?" shouted a man in an orange emergency jumpsuit.

"Ready!" Jake yelled back.

He was currently dangling off the north face of O'Malley's Peak, wind whistling, while his training-partner-slash-victim for this rescue was strapped to a body board.

"Victim's secure for lift."

He sagged into his riggings to wait, enjoying the stunning views from this vantage point. Bright autumn colors dotted the landscape as far as the eye could see, and the city of Anchorage gleamed in the distance. Most tourists cleared out of Chugach State Park this late in the season, leaving it to year-round locals like himself until the first snows hit. Then this place would be packed again, with ice-climbers, skiers and winter enthusiasts.

And, like clockwork, some of those weekend daredevils would do something ill-advised, requiring intervention. That was why he was here. Plus, volunteering for the Anchorage Rescue Team—or the ART—helped him keep his rescue skills sharp. And, particularly this weekend, he hoped the training might help him forget about a certain blond doctor who seemed to haunt his every waking moment.

Dr. Molly Flynn was proving to be a challenge. In more ways than one.

Inhaling the crisp mountain air, Jake distracted himself by double-checking both his harness and the one around his pretend victim, then tested the ropes and carabiners for strength. He'd scaled these peaks since his teens, knew every nook and cranny by heart. He and his dad had used to come here when he was in high school, just to hang out and relax.

Those carefree days seemed a million miles away now, with his parents off traveling the country by RV for three-quarters of each year, returning to Alaska only during the brief summer months. In fact Bobby was really the closest person he had left in Anchorage.

If I lose him…

Jake's muscles tightened with anxiety. The wind gusted harder and he grabbed the ropes near his victim's chest to steady himself. He wouldn't lose Bobby because he couldn't lose Bobby. Just as he couldn't allow himself to get involved with Dr. Flynn. It would be bad. Very bad. Besides, he didn't trust her—would never trust her. Kellie had destroyed his ability to trust.

"You trying to cop a feel, Doc?" Wendy Smith—fellow ART volunteer, an ER nurse at Anchorage Mercy and today's pretend victim—grinned up at him from the body board. "Been there, done that—not going back again."

"Shut up, smartass." Jake focused on the distant hazy peaks of Denali, doing his best to shake off his melancholy. He and Wendy had known each other since grade school. "You have a rare day off too, Clutch?"

"Don't call me that. I hate it," she said.

Half-Inupiat and all attitude, Wendy looked like a swimsuit model, swore like a drunken drill sergeant, and had grown up fast after her mother had passed away when she was only twelve.

Living with three older brothers and having a mechanic

for a father had made her into quite a tomboy, and Jake often found her tinkering with cars when she wasn't saving lives in his ER. They'd gone out once, but the romantic sparks hadn't been there. They'd remained good friends ever since.

"And I could ask the same of you," she said.

"What?" He scowled. "I take plenty of time off."

"Right."

"I can't help it if my patients need me."

She gave him an exasperated look. "Whatever gets you through the night."

He squirmed a bit. Her comment had hit too close to home. Trouble was, his time-honored excuse wasn't getting him through the night anymore. Especially since a certain prickly and disturbingly pretty media star had arrived.

They were totally unsuited. Polar opposites on so many levels it wasn't even funny. His best bet would be to put her out of his mind and concentrate on Bobby's recovery. Except all it seemed to take was one thought of her and his blood burned like lit gasoline, sparking a primal rush of need he didn't expect or want.

Jake peered up toward the summit, waiting for the signal to start his ascent. Finally their new field commander waved, giving the all clear, and he started the slow pull-stop-readjust-pull-stop-readjust that would hoist them back to civilization. His muscles strained and the excess adrenaline clawing through his system began to burn off with the effort.

Undeterred by the fact that she was supposed to be comatose, Wendy continued to chatter. "I hear you're working with a celebrity."

"Excuse me?" Jake muttered a curse as a particularly stiff carabiner gave him issues.

"That fancy doctor from the television show. Hot stuff, from what the orderlies say."

Frowning, Jake maneuvered them around a rock ledge.

For some reason the thought of other men talking about Dr. Flynn made him want to punch something. "Which ones?"

"Pretty much every straight single male working at Anchorage Mercy."

Wendy shrugged, causing the body board to sway precariously. Jake gave her a warning glare.

"The ones I talked to said they wouldn't mind showing her some Alaskan hospitality…"

Between the strong breeze and Wendy's observations, this ascent was becoming more treacherous by the second. The fact that Jake had stayed up far later than he should have researching Molly Flynn's credentials last night probably didn't help either. Nor did the fact that Dr. Dave had been right, dammit. Dr. Flynn was brilliant—but such over-achievement came at a price.

In his experience, high intelligence like hers meant spending all your time with your nose stuck in a book, not connecting with people. One more difference between them—which only made his ever-growing attraction to her that much more baffling.

"Dr. Flynn's only interested in her case and her show—that's it."

"Real workaholic, huh?" Wendy shoved her hand in the pocket of her jumpsuit. "Sounds like someone else I know."

"I'm not a workaholic. I have other interests, hobbies. Look at me now."

"Yes. Dancing on a knife's edge is so relaxing, eh? Here."

Jake stared at the oblong ivory-colored object she held out to him. "What's that?"

"A carved walrus tooth—brings the owner luck."

He tucked it safely in his jumpsuit pocket, then worked the carabiners again. "Thanks."

"Any time. My brother Mike's got a whole tent full of them at the State Fair this year. Tourists love them." Wendy winked. "So, you going to ask this woman out or not?"

"Not," Jake said.

As they neared the summit the voices of the ART team grew louder—pretend orders were barked, pretend conversations with the hospital were called in by 911.

From this height, the valley below was even more breathtaking—golden fields, a few mountain goats foraging, the modern skyscrapers of Anchorage shining like golden monoliths in the sunshine, and the sparkling waters of the lagoon and Cook Inlet beyond deep blue and clear. The air zinged with the mossy scent of dead leaves and the cry of a red-tail hawk pierced the sky.

Multiple hands reached down to help Jake get Wendy over the edge of the summit, then assisted him in the last few steps to the top. Once they were both safely on solid ground Jake unhooked the ropes from his harness and felt the last of his pent-up tension dissipate.

Maybe Wendy was right. Not about asking out Dr. Flynn, but at least about getting to know her. After all, they would be stuck working with each other for the next few weeks. Better to be on friendly terms than at one another's throats the whole time. And perhaps the spark of rivalry between them would drive them both to solve Bobby's case.

Sparks…

In an instant his traitorous mind flashed images of he and Dr. Flynn creating an entirely different kind of fire, reaching new heights of passion between the sheets, their limbs tangled, his hands in her hair, his mouth on her skin, his name on her lips as he brought her to the brink of ecstasy…

Jake cursed under his breath and ran a hand through his wind-tousled hair. He had to stop thinking about Dr. Flynn that way. They were working on a case together. She'd be gone in a few weeks. He'd be stuck here alone. Again. It was too complicated.

Dr. Flynn was here for Bobby. He couldn't allow himself to go down that path again, to be vulnerable. He couldn't. Jake took a deep breath and scanned the area, spotting the

ART vehicles, a burgundy-colored Range Rover, and a cameraman with his lens pointed directly at…

Oh. Hell. No.

He stalked over to where the woman foremost in his thoughts stood with her crew. "What's going on?" Jake demanded. "Why are you here?"

"Good to see you again, Dr. Ryder." Dr. Flynn's producer, Neal, extended his hand. "We've been out all morning getting exterior shots. One of your nurses gave us a tip about this practice drill today. We figured we'd take advantage of the beautiful scenery and the excitement."

"Must be fun…cavorting around while Bobby's in his hospital bed." Jake's gaze never left Dr. Flynn.

Color slowly flushed her cheeks. "I do not cavort and I'm on call with the staff twenty-four-seven." She gave him a cursory glance. "What's your excuse, Dr. Ryder?"

"This is my day off—not that it's any of your business." Jake had intended to be brusque, except the nearer he got, the more he caught Dr. Flynn's scent—light, floral, like sunshine and happiness. He clenched his fists at his sides.

This was ridiculous. He shouldn't want to touch her. And yet he did. So much it hurt. His fingertips itched with the crazy urge to stroke her skin, to see if it felt as velvety as it looked. His lips tingled with the insane need to taste her. His heart thudded, drowning out every other sound in the area but her voice.

Summoning every ounce of willpower he possessed, Jake stepped back, turning to Neal once more. "You said one of my nurses gave you a tip that we'd be out here today. Who?"

"Her." The cameraman, Rob, pointed. "Over there."

Wendy waved innocently as the ART crew trundled her off to the MediVac unit.

Jake stared at the departing chopper, perplexed. Wendy, of all people, knew of his aversion to the limelight—knew what had happened with Kellie and how he didn't want to get involved like that again. Why would she push him?

Scowling, he refocused on Neal. "If you have any shots of me your footage is useless. No releases, remember?"

"Don't worry," Rob said. "I shot around you."

"We don't want to get sued any more than you want your privacy invaded, Dr. Ryder," Neal said.

"There are worse things than having people want to get to know you better," Dr. Molly Flynn said, still not looking at him.

"Really?" Jake kept his distance and jammed his hands into his pockets, in case he got the overwhelming urge to touch her again. "And what might they be?"

For a brief second pain flickered through her gaze, so fast he would've missed it if he hadn't been watching her so intently. The edges of Dr. Flynn's lips tightened, causing his well-guarded heart to tug.

"No one knowing the real you at all."

Her tone held such sadness that Jake had to force himself not to ask more. Whatever the woman's issues were, he'd do best to steer clear of them. No good could come from forming an attachment to her. He had a busy life—no time for a relationship, and no time for what would surely be nothing but heartbreak in the end.

With a curt nod, Jake re-joined the rest of the ART team to help them pack up the gear, reminding himself for the umpteenth time of his goals for the next few weeks. He'd work with Dr. Flynn to consult on Bobby's case—always off-camera—and monitor his best buddy's progress.

Forget this awareness that flared brighter than a supernova. Forget this wayward attraction. Forget his raging pulse and the way the world came alive whenever she was around.

That was the best option. The safe option. The smart option.

Now, if Jake could remember those things whenever they were together, he'd be all set.

CHAPTER FOUR

TWO DAYS PASSED with no further sign of Dr. Jake Ryder, though Gladys had let Molly know he'd stopped by each day to see Bobby. True to his word, he'd avoided both her and her crew like the plague. And, given all the weird reactions he evoked inside her whenever he was around, that was fine. Also, considering the fact she hadn't made any real progress on the Templeton file, Molly didn't need any distractions.

All Bobby's tests had been negative. Even the chest CT had showed no vascular problems, so no Churg-Strauss. Good for the patient, bad for Molly—since she had nothing else to go on at present.

She slumped in the hard plastic chair in her tiny interim office and sighed. Cases had stumped her before, but never one like this.

Stretching her aching neck and back, Molly stared up at the ceiling. She hadn't slept much since she'd been here, which wasn't uncommon. New hotel, new bed, new noises to wake her every hour or so… About the time she got used to her surroundings it would be time to leave again and head home. But at least she hadn't received any more surprise phone calls from her mother. Or hurtful texts from Brian.

Molly yawned, then winced at the stiffness in her muscles. Maybe she should've taken Gladys up on the second cup of coffee she'd offered earlier.

The familiar voices of her crew filtered in through the open office door. Today Neal and Rob were shooting filler scenes and staff interviews for the show, in between documenting the patient's many tests and visitors. All in all, the whole trip thus far had been a lesson in patience and persistence instead of the rousing ratings booster the network had envisioned.

Pushing to her feet and stretching, Molly was just about to head out and grab some lunch in the cafeteria when the overhead PA system crackled to life.

"Dr. Flynn to ICU Room 407, stat. Paging Dr. Flynn to ICU 407, stat."

That was Bobby's room.

She raced for the door. Nurses were pushing trays of equipment in the same direction and Molly broke into a jog. Rob and Neal were already waiting by the door when she arrived. She elbowed her way through the small crowd, concerned. Bobby had been doing fine when she'd checked on him an hour earlier.

"Stand back, please."

Molly shoved the privacy curtain aside. Bobby sat on his bed, arms crossed and face contorted with fear, huddled in a corner of the mattress, staring up at the ceiling in horror. She checked the monitors—his vitals appeared normal.

"He's delirious," Gladys said, shooing the other people out of the room. "Keeps mumbling about the enemy on the roof and people creeping through the walls."

Leaning closer to her patient, Molly put her hand on his arm—only to feel his whole body stiffen.

Bobby collapsed onto the bed, convulsing. "He's seizing!"

"What's going on?" Dr. Ryder yelled as he burst into the room. "I got here as fast as I could."

Molly waved him over to the bed. "Help me get him on his side."

He rushed over and helped turn his friend. "Whoa. That rash is new."

"What rash?" She frowned down at the red blisters covering the patient's left lower leg. "Gladys, is this his first seizure?"

"Yes, Doctor."

The patient's body relaxed and Molly released Bobby's weight onto the mattress. "Any signs of fever prior?"

"No, Doctor."

Bobby blinked open his eyes and seemed genuinely shocked to find them all staring at him. "Why's everybody watching me?"

"Everything will be fine, Mr. Templeton. Don't panic." Molly gave him her best reassuring smile. "You had a seizure. Do you remember anything about what happened?"

"No. All I recall is speaking to the nurse, then things got fuzzy."

"Okay." She took his file from Gladys. "I'll get to the bottom of this, I promise. Let the nurse finish checking your vitals, then we'll talk again."

Dr. Ryder swore and looked away, but not before Molly caught the deep worry in his eyes. It was the same concern burrowing deep inside her.

"I'm going to speak with Dr. Flynn for a moment and I'll be back," he told Bobby.

"Sure." Bobby tucked the robe tightly around himself again. "Just please someone find out what's wrong with me."

Molly exited the room, Dr. Ryder hot on her heels. Her mind raced with new information, quickening her steps.

"He was delirious right before you arrived. Talked about people being up on the roof and men creeping through the walls. Do you know anything about that?"

They entered her office seconds later and Dr. Ryder closed the door behind them. "I still think it could be encephalitis. Did you get a lumbar puncture?"

"I did. This morning. Waiting on results."

Molly took a seat behind her desk and opened the folder, not missing the fact that he'd avoided her question. But she had bigger problems to solve first.

"Those vesicles on his leg look like herpes."

"If it is herpetic encephalitis, then his immune system is severely compromised."

Dr. Ryder leaned over her shoulder, unlooping the stethoscope from around his neck and placing it on Molly's desk as he stared at his friend's chart. His warmth surrounded her again, carrying along with it a hint of the crisp outdoors, reminding her of their last meeting on top of O'Malley's Peak. He'd been angry with her for being there, but there'd also been a lingering spark of want in his eyes. Just like that first night at the accident scene. An answering need coiled tight inside her before Molly tamped it down.

"Steroids suppress the immune system, but not to this degree, so it can't be the medication." She called the nurses' station. "Gladys, start Mr. Templeton on IV acyclovir: twelve hundred milligrams every eight hours for the next ten days."

Molly hung up, then peered at Jake over her shoulder, resisting the urge to snuggle against him.

"The drug is relatively non-toxic. Empirical treatment is recommended by the ADA."

"No argument here."

"That's a first."

"Don't worry. I'm sure we'll find something to disagree on momentarily."

He winked, and her stomach fluttered despite her solemn intent to steer clear of him.

Dr. Ryder held Molly's gaze for a long moment, his lips so close that if she leaned in an inch more they'd kiss…

Dr. Ryder cleared his throat and stepped back, returning his attention to the file, a hint of color flushing his high cheekbones. His words emerged a bit huskier than before—another sign that she wasn't the only one affected by this powerful connection between them.

"The herpes diagnosis still bothers me, though," he said, rubbing his hand over the back of his neck. "Seems too easy. What about Lupus? Bobby said he felt better on the steroids. That could explain why."

"Except the treatment for Lupus would be more steroids,

which we can't use if it's encephalitis." Molly forced the words past her constricted throat. "I'll…uh…make sure the network edits you out of those shots."

"Oh, yeah." His dark brows drew together, as if he'd only just now remembered her crew had been filming back in Bobby's room.

He licked his lips and she wondered if his mouth tasted as good as it looked. Molly lowered her gaze and clasped her hands tight in her lap. She'd never felt so turned on, or so torn. Her father would have a field-day if he could see her, acting like a hormonal teenager. Good thing he was thousands of miles away in China.

Dr. Ryder headed for the door. "I'll check in on Bobby later."

Perhaps it was the adrenaline still pumping through her system, or her complete lack of common sense at that moment, but Molly didn't want him to leave just yet.

"What did Bobby mean the other day when he said you felt like you had to watch out for him?"

"Huh?" Dr. Ryder swiveled to face her again, his expression guarded.

Dazed, Molly met his eyes and saw a deep loneliness and yearning to match her own. This crazy bond between them reminded her of a runaway train, rumbling headlong down the tracks toward what she feared was certain disaster. If she didn't move, didn't avoid it at all costs, it would sweep her right off the map…

Luckily Dr. Ryder stayed where he was, half in, half out of her office, allowing Molly to regain some semblance of control over herself. Whatever this was sparking between them was best forgotten. It was probably nothing. Except, given the way her heart jackhammered against her ribcage just from his nearness, it certainly felt like…something.

Flustered, Molly shook her head to clear it. "You two served in the military together, correct? Dr. Dave told me you've done several tours as a combat medic in Afghanistan and Bobby was on your security team. Perhaps—"

"I doubt our time in the Army is relevant." Dr. Ryder scraped a hand through his hair, his usually smooth movements agitated. "I need to get back to my ER. Let me know when those test results come in."

"Will do." She watched him leave, feeling oddly bereft— which was silly. They were coworkers, that was all.

To get her mind off the awareness still bubbling through her Molly got back to work, scribbling details of Bobby's new symptoms and treatment plan in his chart. But when she went to turn the page her movement was blocked by Dr. Ryder's stethoscope.

He'll need that.

She'd been on her way to the cafeteria earlier, so it wouldn't be out of her way to drop it off. Not to mention she'd have a chance to observe him in his natural environment—maybe figure out what made him tick.

Decision made, Molly headed for the elevators, stethoscope in hand.

"Hey, Mol!" Neal yelled from the other end of the hall. "We need to get some follow-up footage."

"In a minute," she called. "I have to take care of a few things first."

Jake walked through the automatic sliding glass doors into the hectic ER, grabbing a chart off the rack and reading it while he headed toward Trauma Bay One. With the first days of October in full swing, and employee vacations galore, he found himself filling in more than ever.

Unwanted sexual heat still shimmered through his blood, and he wasn't sure if it was the mental rush of running diagnoses with Dr. Flynn or the flood of need that washed over him whenever he was around her. But if he hadn't moved away when he had, he would've kissed her. Would probably still be kissing her now, given the yearning thrum-ming inside him.

And that would be stupid. He barely knew her, let alone trusted her. Kissing Dr. Flynn would be a monumental mis-take.

Jake took a deep breath and double-checked the name on the file before heading past the drawn curtain. "Hello, Ms. Murphy. I'm Dr. Ryder. What brings you in to see us today?"

The portly senior citizen pointed at the two EMTs stand-ing near the corner of the room—Zac and a new girl from the local volunteer fire department named Stacy—and gave the pair a disgruntled look. "They made me come."

"They did?" Jake grinned at the paramedics. "What hap-pened?"

Ms. Murphy reached through the bedside rail and clasped his hand, her voice a whisper. "You see, I had to use the restroom."

"Okay…" He glanced at Zac, who kept his expression blank. "Then what?"

"Well, I couldn't get up."

"Her knees buckled," Stacy supplied helpfully.

"Oh, hush. I don't know why I ended up in this place." The patient gave Zac and Stacy another dirty look before continuing. "Hey, Doc. You're handsome. You remind me of that guy in those superhero movies. What's his name? Captain somebody?"

"Thanks." Jake smiled. "I'll take that as a compliment."

"You should." Ms. Murphy batted her eyelashes.

Stacy stepped forward. "She became nauseated…vom-ited a little too."

"Okay." He jotted a few notes on the patient's chart. "When you were in the bathroom did you experience any chest pain, Ms. Murphy?"

"No."

"How about feeling like you were going to pass out?"

"Yes." The woman's gaze widened. "I suffer from sciatica. My back was killing me."

"I'm sorry to hear that."

More than likely it had been the patient's nerve issues causing her problems. Still, he needed to run the proper tests to rule out something more serious, like a stroke.

Jake sent Zac and Stacy on their way, then turned to Ms. Murphy again. "All right, I'm going to—"

"Oh, I'm sorry."

Jake's heart skipped a crazy beat as Dr. Flynn came around the curtain, his stethoscope in her hand.

"The nurse at the station said to come on in. You left this in my office."

"Thanks." The word creaked past his tight vocal cords.

All he had to do was take the stethoscope and let her walk away. Temptation avoided. Only he couldn't seem to do it—because he was a weak-willed idiot where she was concerned.

"I…uh…appreciate that."

His fingers brushed Dr. Flynn's as he took his stethoscope, sending an electric jolt of lust straight through him. He met her startled gaze and discovered an answering passion. Oh, boy. This was going to be difficult. Difficult because everything about her drew him in like a moth to a flame—her quirky shy smile, her focus on work instead of on the persona the network had built, her beautiful brain and the equally stunning package it came in.

Do not go there.

At least some part of Jake's rational mind still seemed to be functioning, sending up alarm bells. Dr. Molly Flynn was off-limits. He reminded himself why he was leery of the media, why he didn't trust his heart or his emotions, why he didn't want to get involved with anyone.

"Hello, there." The overt curiosity in Ms. Murphy's voice had Jake snapping to attention. "What's your name, honey?"

Dr. Flynn gave him a deer-in-the-headlights look, frozen in place. "Uh… Molly Flynn."

"I've got a granddaughter named Molly in New York. Come closer, so I can see you properly. Just look at that skin, Dr. Ryder. Creamy and smooth."

Pink color suffused Dr. Flynn's cheeks and Jake gripped the chart tighter, continued to advise the patient of his treatment plan.

"As I was saying, Ms. Murphy, I'll order some bloodwork and a few scans to make sure there are no blockages or bleeding. If all those come back okay, then we'll discuss your living arrangements."

At eighty-four, the woman was at too high a risk to live alone if she was unstable on her feet. The last thing Jake wanted was to send the poor lady home only to have her return with a broken hip or worse.

While he jotted down orders for Wendy, Ms. Murphy tugged a hesitant Dr. Flynn closer. For someone who made her living in the public eye, Bobby's new physician seemed decidedly wary of attention—hardly the media darling Jake had expected. In fact, Dr. Flynn was different in a lot of ways from what he'd expected.

"You're not married, are you?" Ms. Murphy said, studying his colleague's ringless left hand. Jake did his best to stifle a grin at Dr. Flynn's obvious discomfort. "This handsome man is available. You two should—"

"I'm not interested in dating," they both said in unison.

Taking that as his cue to leave, Jake headed toward the exit—only to be halted by his patient's voice. "Wait a minute, Dr. Ryder. I just want to stretch my legs a bit…"

He swiveled to see Ms. Murphy teetering on her feet. The older lady swayed for a moment before falling forward—straight toward Dr. Flynn. She rushed forward at the same moment Jake dived, and they ended up locked in an awkward hug, with the patient sandwiched in between them like an overstuffed hoagie.

"This isn't quite how I pictured my afternoon going," Dr. Flynn said, her voice muffled by a face full of hospital gown.

"No?" Jake leaned around Ms. Murphy's side to meet her gaze. "Working in the ER, you come to expect the unexpected."

"I should have remembered."

"Ready on three?" he asked.

Together they managed to get the patient safely back into bed.

Afterward, shoulders stiff and neck sore, Jake stood beside Dr. Flynn at the end of Ms. Murphy's bed. If he'd had a hard time with the patient's bulk, he couldn't imagine the toll on Molly Flynn's petite frame.

"Are you okay?" he whispered.

A stray lock of hair had come loose from the tight bun at the nape of Dr. Flynn's neck. Before Jake could second-guess his actions he'd tucked it behind her ear. Yep. Her flushed skin felt like silk beneath his touch, and his wayward thoughts quickly transitioned to whether she blushed that beautifully in other…situations.

"I'm fine." She sidled away, avoiding his gaze. "Are you all right, Ms. Murphy?"

"I'm great, kiddo." The patient gave them both a saucy wink.

Considering the older woman's quick wits, Jake wouldn't have put it past her to fall on purpose. It seemed everyone was a matchmaker these days.

Ms. Murphy grinned. "Promise me you'll find yourself a nice man and have lots of beautiful babies, okay?"

Dr. Flynn frowned. "I'm focused on my career and…"

"Nonsense." Ms. Murphy scoffed. "You can be a doctor and a mother and anything else you want to be." Her gaze darted between the two of them. "Besides, with this fine hunk of superhero around you'd be a fool not to take advantage."

"Don't mind her, Dr. Flynn," Jake said, feeling an unaccountable urge to put her at ease.

"Under the circumstances, Dr. Ryder," she said. "I think you can call me Molly."

Given their rather rocky start, he hadn't expected that, and it knocked him off his game, making him stumble over his words. "Oh, right. Sure. And…uh…you can call me Jake."

"Go, love!" Ms. Murphy gave them two thumbs-up as a technician arrived to take her away. "Don't do anything I wouldn't."

The gurney rolled past and Jake gave Molly a quick side glance, finding that same piece of hair had slipped free to dangle against her cheek. Time slowed as he reached out to brush it behind her ear again…

"I need to go." Molly scurried from the room faster than scorpions in the Kandahar desert.

Go. Yep. Jake needed to go too. Go and get his head on straight before he did something insane like haul Molly into his arms and kiss her senseless.

CHAPTER FIVE

"A HYPERBARIC CHAMBER?" Dr. Dave said, his tone incredulous.

Molly stood across from him, with Bobby's bed between them and her crew rolling. They'd been at Anchorage Mercy for a week and a half and she finally had an inkling as to what might be wrong with her patient. Now, if she could just get the chief of staff to sign off on the testing, she'd have firm confirmation.

"Yes. It's a bit unconventional, but do you have one?"

"Well, of course." Dr. Dave frowned. "We keep one in the Burn Unit to aid in wound healing, but I don't see how that would help in this situation."

She walked around to stand beside the older man, lowering her voice to avoid waking Bobby, who'd managed to fall asleep at last. "Let's talk in the hall."

They exited the room and Rob followed with his camera.

"I received the patient's latest lab results early this morning," Molly said, once they'd reached a deserted spot near the end of the corridor. "He tested positive for herpetic encephalitis."

Dr. Dave winced. "I told that boy to be careful with all those groupies."

"Sexual transmission isn't the only way to transmit the virus. And, regardless of how he acquired it, the results still point to one thing."

"Which is?"

"His immune system is severely compromised."

"Oh." Dr. Dave stared out the nearby window, then back at Molly again. "His file says we prescribed steroids early on…"

"Yes, but two doses of medication wouldn't cause something this bad." Dr. Dave's tense shoulders relaxed and Molly sighed. "I think we need to look at other possible diagnoses."

"Such as?"

"Mixed Connective Tissue Disorder. It explains most of his symptoms. It would also explain why the patient felt better while on the steroids, at least initially." She closed the file and took a deep breath. "That's why a hyperbaric chamber is our best and only option."

"I still don't see the link." Dr. Dave shook his head. "Sorry."

"The normal treatment for MCTD is corticosteroids, but we can't use them for obvious reasons."

Rob moved in closer for a tight shot.

"Therefore we need to treat him with something that modulates the immune system but doesn't suppress it."

"I don't know…" Dr. Dave paced the narrow corridor. "There's no established protocol for using hyperbaric treatments for autoimmune disorders and it's not without risks. What about oxygen toxicity or damage to his eyes or liver?"

"Those risks are minimal compared to the greater benefits of this treatment."

"Well, if you think it's the best way…"

"I do." Molly put an arm around Dr. Dave and led him back toward the elevators. "Now, do you need to book the sessions with the Burn Unit or shall I?"

"And…cut!" Neal's voice echoed down the hall.

Dr. Dave made the necessary call, then turned back to Molly with a smile. "I have a surprise."

She held her breath. Surprises—in her world, at least—weren't good things.

"Your father will be in Anchorage this Sunday. Turns out he's been asked to consult on a transplant case up at Fairbanks General and he called me to say he's going to fly in here from Beijing, then drive north. He's looking forward to seeing you. We'll talk later."

Molly forced a smile and headed back toward Bobby's room.

My father. Here. In three days.

Nausea and dread knotted into a tight ball inside her stomach. He might be consulting on a case, but the only reason he'd stop in Anchorage would be to keep an eye on his disappointment of a daughter—plain and simple. Most likely because he couldn't stand the fact that Molly was breaking out on her own after all this time.

She was still stewing over her father's impending visit when Jake burst out of the nearby stairwell a few minutes later, his expression dark.

"Are you filming?" he asked.

"No. We just finished. Why?" She gave him a confused look. "What's going on?"

"We need to talk. In private."

"Follow me."

Molly took him into the small meditation chapel, finally releasing the breath she'd been holding. It had been nearly five days since she'd seen him in the ER, but his effect on her was still as potent. Her pulse sped and her knees wobbled.

"What's happening?"

"You can't give Bobby hyperbaric treatments."

Molly frowned. "How'd you hear about that? Dr. Dave only just called in the order."

"I've got friends in the Burn Unit." Jake rubbed his eyes, as if struggling for patience. "Bobby's a hockey player— a professional athlete. If the chamber damages his lungs, his career's over."

"But it's the best option at this point with MCTD."

Molly's annoyance levels rose along with her unaccountable awareness of this man's every move, his every touch, his every breath. Not to mention she wasn't used to having her orders on a case questioned.

He braced his arm against the wall beside her head and his masculine presence seemed to envelop her. It was enough to drive her batty. That and the fact that the guy seemed to have friends everywhere. Or spies. Either way, she doubted the bullet trains in Japan worked as fast as the rumor mill here at Anchorage Mercy.

Jake narrowed his gaze. "You don't even know if that's what's wrong," he said, his tone skeptical. "I saw the blood-work. His ANAs were barely elevated."

"Bobby's still my patient, and I feel this is the best course of action." Molly tapped the toe of her shoe against the shiny linoleum, wanting to throttle him and cuddle him in equal measure. Which made no logical sense.

The stress over her father's impending appearance mingled with Molly's untenable, undeniable attraction to this irritating man who challenged her at every step and boiled over into simmering fury. How dared he question her methods? Distracting her with his looks and his charm and his potent, provocative…steaminess.

She matched his guarded pose and raised her chin defiantly. "What about his underlying condition?"

"There is no underlying condition."

"Oh, yes, there is."

Molly pointed out several lab results, which Jake brushed off as coincidental. God, he was the most infuriating male she'd ever met. To think she'd considered kissing him a minute ago. She'd rather kiss a toad at this point.

Exhaling slowly, to regain her control, Molly considered her options. She could continue arguing with him about this, which would only waste time and effort. She could concede to his wishes and forget about the hyperbaric chamber completely. Or she could compromise—strike a bargain that would only prove her point in the end.

"Fine. We'll try your treatment first. If there's no improvement by next week, we do things my way."

"Fine. All I want is Bobby healthy again."

"And what do you think I want? Don't you think I want him to get well?"

Jake stared at her, unblinking, his expression unreadable. For a moment he looked as if he wanted to say more, do more. His fingers curled and uncurled at his sides and his gaze flickered to her lips again before returning to her eyes.

"Honestly, I don't know what you want, Molly. That's the problem."

With that, he yanked open the chapel door and stalked out. Molly took a few solitary moments to calm her raging pulse before heading back to Gladys's desk. Her heart ached as much from their argument as from the passionate heat sparking between them.

Molly plunked Bobby's chart down on the counter, resisting the urge to fan her burning cheeks. "Change of plan for Mr. Templeton. Hyperbaric treatments are on hold. Instead, let's start him on forty percent oxygen until his O_2 sats increase and prescribe him a non-steroidal anti-inflammatory."

Jake got the page on his way back down to the ER, his posture tense and his blood pounding as he leaned against the elevator wall.

Gunshot victim. ETA ten minutes.

He was on a much-needed break, meaning his team would only call him back in if the situation was dire. Work usually settled him, but his senses were rioting. And unfortunately he knew exactly what had caused it—or rather who.

Bad enough that each time he saw Molly these days all he seemed to focus on was her soft skin, her sweet, distracting scent, her pink full lips. Lord help him. A man could drown in that mouth and die happy.

Focus, Ryder. Focus.

He spent too much time alone these days—that had to be the problem. Since Bobby had gotten sick, most nights when Jake wasn't in the ER he was at home, working on the never-ending renovations to his place. The truth was, he liked using his hands, and it felt good to make something, to create something lasting. After all the destruction he'd witnessed during the war, building felt pretty damned amazing.

Jake shifted his weight, pulling out his phone again to check for updates as the doors opened and he hurried toward his department. Wendy met him at the glass doors and walked with him into the controlled chaos of the ER, handing him a scrub jacket and hat as they headed for the ambulance entrance.

"What's the cause of the shooting?"

"Not sure yet," she said. "All we've got so far from the EMT crew is that the wound's in the left flank and the patient's breath is agonal."

Gasping for air meant dropping oxygen levels. Jake cringed. "Exit wound?"

"None the paramedics could find."

"Damn. We'll need to order a CT to locate the bullet."

He finished tying his mask just as the ambulance crew wheeled the patient down the ramp from the helicopter pad and into the ER.

"Give it to me," Jake said to Zac, jogging next to the gurney as they veered off toward Trauma Bay Two, a team of nurses and technicians following.

"Nineteen-year-old male, hunting accident. Single bullet hole in the left side."

"Okay." Jake waited while the patient was transferred to the trauma bay table then patted the kid's cheeks. "Sir? Can you tell me your name?"

Nothing.

He tried again, louder and more forcefully, pinching the guy this time as well. It seemed harsh, but they had to rouse him if they could.

"Sir? Tell me your name."

No response.

Nineteen was too young to die, and Jake refused to let it happen on his watch.

"All right, team, we need an O2 sat. He's not responding to painful stimuli; GCS is less than seven. Get ready to intubate for airway protection."

While one of his residents moved in to insert a tracheal tube, Jake continued his rundown of the patient's vitals.

"Agonal breathing indicates a lack of oxygen and a seven on the Glasgow Coma Scale suggests a strong possibility of traumatic brain injury."

"We're in." The resident withdrew the bronchoscope and Wendy used the clear plastic tube to pump air directly into the patient's lungs.

Jake continued his exam. "Nothing in the axilla areas. Bilateral breath sounds. Only one visible wound in the left lower lateral chest wall. Blood pressure down to sixty-nine over forty-two. Okay, people. Let's move this to the OR. We need to find where that bullet landed."

While his team took the patient upstairs by elevator, Jake discarded his soiled jacket and mask in a nearby biohazard bin, then hustled to the stairwell. The kid had lost a lot of blood and his pulse was weak. Time was of the essence.

As he jogged upstairs memories of his time in the military swamped him. He'd joined right after graduating from medical school and proposing to Kellie.

She'd been two years behind him in college, so once he'd got out of the service after six years and returned stateside she'd been established at the local network affiliate as a reporter. She'd suggested putting off marriage a little longer, to let things settle and get back to normal after the media frenzy over his Distinguished Service Cross commendation. At the time, it had seemed like the right thing to do.

But the longer they'd put off the wedding, the more the relationship had started to unravel. Kellie had resented his long hours at the hospital and claimed he'd changed since the war. He'd disliked her newfound love of the spotlight and constant craving for attention.

In the end it had all gone horribly wrong.

Jake pushed out through the second-floor doorway and hurried over to the prep area. It didn't matter. All that mattered tonight was saving this kid's life.

He scrubbed down with Betadine, then backed into the OR, arms bent and raised at the elbow to prevent contamination. A surgical nurse outfitted him in a fresh jacket and mask. The anesthesiologist finished administering the required dosage of sedative and Jake approached the operating table.

Talking through his actions always helped him stay centered and focused during complex cases. Bobby had used to tease him when they were out on desert rescues.

"You gonna save them, Doc, or talk them to death…?"

Today, hopefully, it would be the former.

He grabbed a scalpel from a nearby tray and made his initial incision.

"Okay, team. We don't know the location of the bullet. Three full-body X-rays found nothing." Jake glanced at the monitors and his own pulse stumbled. "We've got to locate the source of the bleeding and clamp it."

Trauma surgery required split-second decisions. Hesitation could mean the difference between life and death.

"The heart's unstable, and the left lung is compromised. Removing it is the only chance we have of saving him."

Jake hated taking such a drastic step on a young kid, but surviving with lowered lung capacity was better than the alternative.

The bullet had ricocheted inside the kid's body, tearing through tissue and complicating matters. It took another hour to complete the delicate surgery, but afterward the patient's blood pressure had stabilized and his pulse strengthened.

Jake stepped away, confident he'd made the right choice. "He's alive. Thanks, everyone."

Wendy followed him out of the OR.

"What are his chances of survival?" she asked as she pulled off her jacket.

"Too early to say." Jake disposed of his soiled gear. "I did what I could, but we still have no idea of the bullet's location. That CT's paramount, but we can't risk moving the kid again until he's stabilized, which could be several hours."

As he washed up and splashed cool water on his face, images of Molly standing toe-to-toe with him in that chapel, giving as good as she got, burned into his mind. Crisis had a way of making everything seem more intense, and between their earlier encounter and the dramatic surgery, Jake felt lucky he didn't have adrenaline poisoning.

It was a good thing he'd gotten away from Molly when he had, or there was no telling what might've happened. He might've cupped those lovely cheeks of hers and kissed her until neither one of them had wanted to argue anymore. He might've pressed her close and relished the feel of her curves against him at last. He might've fallen to his knees and begged for one night in her arms.

Lord, help me.

Jake dried his face with a scratchy white towel, then tossed it into the bin with the rest of the soiled items before rolling his stiff shoulders. "I'm going to the gym for the rest of my break. Keep me posted on the patient's status."

CHAPTER SIX

AFTER HOURS OF nonstop reviewing of medical journals for clues to her patient's condition, Molly blinked to clear the blurriness from her vision and finally admitted she needed a break. Normally this late at night she'd hit the workout facility at her hotel and then go to bed, but she didn't want to leave the hospital just yet. There were still a few test results pending for Bobby, and she wanted to wait until they came back before she left.

She recalled seeing an employee gym in the basement of the hospital, on one of her many trips to the cafeteria. Back home in Chicago she ran five miles a day and kick-boxed to stay in shape. Here, she sat in her tiny office most of the time and drank ultra-strong coffee. Stiff and achy, Molly pushed to her feet and grabbed her duffle bag from the corner.

Time to get her mojo back.

She took the elevator down to the brightly lit basement and followed the overhead signs to the staff locker room. After changing into a pair of yoga pants and a tank, Molly headed out into the gym area.

The whole place looked empty, except for one guy jogging on a treadmill near the back wall. He had earbuds in and his shirt off, clearly in the zone as sweat trickled down his tanned torso and toned back. He was in fantastic shape. Cute too, with dark, damp hair spiked around his head.

As Molly neared the short row of treadmills, however, her heart sank. It was Jake, jogging along, eyes closed, seemingly oblivious to her presence.

She tossed her towel over to the wall, then climbed aboard the only other treadmill machine, on the left of

Jake's. Okay, fine. If she was quiet, perhaps he wouldn't even notice she was there.

Faint strains of music pumped from his earbuds, increasing her sense of security. With his volume that loud, Mt. St. Helene's could erupt again and he wouldn't know.

Except, as Molly set up her running course and pressed "Start," she couldn't seem to keep her attention from drifting over to Jake's reflection in the mirrors, her blood sizzling anew at the remembered feel of his fingertips against her skin, the scent of his skin, the deep rumble of his voice as they'd argued in the chapel.

Her gaze flicked down his body—all lean, corded muscle and sinewy strength. A tattoo covered his left bicep. She squinted. A caduceus, maybe?

Molly glanced up again and found him watching her, his expression wary. Uh-oh. He pulled out his earbuds and gave her a tiny half-smile. Or was that a frown? Hard to tell when all she seemed able to focus on was the bead of sweat gliding down the side of his neck and her sudden longing to lick that moisture, to taste the salt of his skin, to feel his alpha strength...

Alpha strength?

She grabbed hold of the sides of the treadmill to keep from tripping over her own feet as the machine picked up speed. Jeez, the stress must be getting to her more than she'd thought if she was resorting to purple prose about her colleagues. This wasn't like her. Not at all.

Getting on with her run, Molly did her best to focus straight ahead and not pay attention to the weight of Jake's stare burning a hole through her composure. Soon the treadmill speed increased yet again and the base tilted upward, and Molly soon lost herself in the bliss of her racing heart and her pounding feet and the illusion of glorious speed.

"Doing the mountain course, huh?" a deep male voice said, interrupting her fantasy.

Her runner's high vanished and her knees threatened

to buckle beneath the satin timbre of his voice. Molly hazarded another glance over at Jake and saw his machine was at maximum incline. She pushed a bit harder to keep up with him, her competitive streak surging despite her shaking muscles and raging libido.

"Yeah. You too?"

He shrugged and looked away. "I have my own special course set up to match the one I run at Chugach on my days off."

"The state park where we filmed your rescue crew?"

"Yep. Been back there yet?"

"Nope." Once again her speed and trajectory notched higher and she pressed onward despite the burn. "I'm here for my patient, remember?"

Taking in some of the natural wonder of the Alaskan wilderness was on Molly's list of things to do, but only if it didn't interfere with Bobby's case. Work came first. Always. That was the way she liked it, right?

Her chest tightened and her breath puffed harder, her whole body tensing at the horrible sinking feeling that maybe it wasn't.

Maybe it's your father who only cares about his career, not you.

She swiped a hand over her sweaty forehead and checked the timer. Five minutes left. She could do this. Sure, she'd blown past her ideal pulse-rate a long time ago, but what was a little heart attack in the name of success?

Jake's machine beeped and his treadmill gradually lowered to its original flat position before stopping completely. "Well, you know what they say."

Molly hazarded an annoyed stare in his direction, puffing. "No. Please enlighten me."

His slow grin nearly toppled her to the floor. Molly gripped the sides of her treadmill and closed her eyes. Seriously, she needed to get over her wanton infatuation with this guy before someone got hurt. Namely her.

"All work and no play…" Jake walked over to stand beside her machine "…makes Dr. Flynn a very dull girl."

Molly opened her mouth to respond, then hesitated, not wanting to reveal just how close to the truth he'd come. That was why Brian had left her. He'd claimed she was about as interesting as a trip to the DMV. Then again, she'd never really opened up to him, so she only had herself to blame. Her flawed, quirky, weird, dull, fallible self.

Her unlovable self.

Before she knew what was happening, her muscles locked and her feet fumbled. The machine beeped and two strong arms pulled Molly close, to keep her from face-planting on the gym floor. Slowly Jake eased her down to a sitting position, then crouched beside her, his expression a mix of concern and barely concealed amusement.

"Doing okay there?" he asked.

"I'm fine."

Her voice sounded shaky even to her own ears. Molly kept her head bent between her knees to increase circulation to her fuzzy brain and to hide her embarrassment.

"I'm used to tougher workouts back home. Must be low blood sugar."

"Right…" No mistaking Jake's teasing tone now. "And here I thought you were trying to impress me."

"Impress you?" The words croaked from her parched throat. "I was not—"

"Here, Usain Bolt." He nudged her arm with a cold bottle of water. "Drink this."

Molly swallowed half the contents in two long gulps. As she drank she saw Jake doing the same, and felt a weird, all-consuming need to nuzzle the thudding pulse-point at the base of his neck.

Frazzled, she pushed to her unsteady feet and grabbed her towel. She still had at least an hour before Bobby's last set of test results were due back from the lab, but she couldn't stay where she was. Not with Jake looking like sex on a stick.

She headed to the far side of the room and a pair of punching bags strung from chains in the ceiling. After strapping on a pair of boxing gloves Molly pummeled one of the bags, zeroing all her anger, pain, and frustration into her jabs. There was one for her mother, for making Molly feel like a dried-up old prune. Another for Brian, for dumping her by text message and reinforcing her doubts about herself. And one final blow for her father, for always pushing her, always expecting the impossible, always treating her like she was never, ever enough.

"Hey. Take it easy, Bolt." Jake strapped on a pair of gloves too, then walked behind her bag to steady it. "You're a kickboxer as well, eh?"

"Yep."

Wham, wham, wham.

It should be illegal for a man to be that sweaty and still look that fine. She ignored the soft clenching in her core caused by his nearness.

"Best fighter at my gym."

"Why am I not surprised?" He shook his head as Molly landed a fierce roundhouse kick.

"What's that supposed to mean?"

"Nothing. You just seem a bit…driven."

"Really?" She stepped back and punched one glove into the other, her gaze narrowed. "You're one to talk. Bobby told me he can't remember the last time you took a vacation."

Jake stood before her, his black shorts riding low on his hips and showing off that delectable V of muscles that always drove her wild with lust.

"Bobby should mind his own business." He rubbed his nose. "Spot me, okay?"

He walked to the other bag and Molly held it while Jake threw some impressive left hooks and right upper cuts.

She attempted to make small talk to distract herself from his rippling muscles. "What's your ink?"

"Huh?" He scowled, throwing a fast flurry of punches.

"The tattoo on your arm. What is it?"

"Combat Medic logo." Jake glanced down at his bicep, then performed a perfectly placed crescent kick that knocked Molly back a few steps. "And watch what you say next. The guys and gals from my regiment are like family."

"Oh." The fierce protectiveness in his voice made her envious. She doubted her own kin would ever defend her so staunchly.

Molly recovered her balance with the help of his steadying hand, missing the pressure of his touch as soon as he let her go.

"I guess that explains why you and Bobby are so close."

"That's part of the reason, yeah."

He stripped off his gloves and tossed them aside. Molly did the same, then walked back with him to their towels and water bottles, silent, doing her best not to say something stupid and ruin the tenuous accord that had settled between them.

"I'm surprised you came here to Alaska," Jake said finally, after pulling a black "Anchorage Mercy" T-shirt over his head. The clothes helped, covering all that forbidden flesh. "Doesn't your network usually prefer more glitzy locations?"

"MedStar thought a sports star case would draw in more viewers, so here I am."

"That simple, huh?"

"That simple." Molly wiped her face on her towel then slung it around her neck, her nerve endings on high alert with him sitting so close. "Why are you so against the media?"

"I was raised to keep my head down and stay humble. Doing good should be its own reward. And I've had some bad experiences with reporters in the past."

Jake leaned against the wall beside her, his arm brushing Molly's and sending a fresh explosion of sparks through her system.

"So... Molly Flynn. Daughter of the famous Roger Flynn?"

She cringed, staring across the empty gym. "Yes."

"We spent a whole semester in medical school studying his suture techniques."

She gave a derisive snort and he narrowed his gaze, his expression thoughtful.

"Must be hard, living up to that kind of perfectionism."

"You have no idea." Head lowered, Molly poked the toe of her running shoe into the carpet. "Everything in my household was performance-based. Everything."

"Ouch. I'm sorry."

"For what?"

Outside, the world might be pure chaos, but in here with him all seemed oddly private and safe. But cracks were appearing in the logical wall she'd built to keep him away—the one that told her touching him, tasting him, would be wrong. Jake was so close now that Molly could see the tiny flecks of gold in his stormy gray eyes, and all her practical ideas and reasons evaporated.

"For what must have been a tough childhood," he said, his voice gentle, husky as he leaned closer still.

She didn't move away. "It wasn't like I was abused or anything."

"No." His gaze lowered to her mouth. "But I bet you weren't nurtured either."

"Nurtured?" The invisible cord between them tightened, the word squeezing Molly's heart like an embrace. "N-no. I wasn't."

"Such a pity..." Jake frowned, his lips hovering over hers for a brief second before capturing them in a light kiss.

Warning bells clanged in the back of Molly's mind, telling her this was happening too fast. Telling her she'd only be hurt by this man who saw too much, who fought as fiercely for what he believed in as she did. But instead of pushing Jake away Molly twined her arms around his neck and pulled him closer, craving his taste more than she craved her next breath.

Jake groaned low and slipped one hand around her waist while the other cupped the back of her head as he deepened the kiss. Molly opened her lips, welcoming the gentle sweep of his tongue and his minty, sweet flavor. It was nice and wonderful and...

Over.

Cursing, Jake pulled away and grabbed the cell phone clipped to the waistband of his shorts, blinking down at the screen with a frown. "Sorry. I've got a critically ill patient in the ICU. He's stabilized enough to get a CT scan. They're taking him now."

Still woozy from the emotional hurricane raging inside her, it took Molly a moment to let the words penetrate her haze of lust.

Patient. Critically ill. CT scan.

Work. Yes. That's why I'm here.

Silence fell between them once more as they gathered their supplies. Kissing Jake had probably been a mistake, but Molly couldn't bring herself to regret it as Jake walked across the hall to the men's locker room.

After a quick shower and a change into a fresh set of scrubs, Jake made a beeline for the ER. Each time he licked his lips he still tasted Molly there—sugar and bright lemon, her flavor zinging through his veins like a narcotic. He'd dropped his guard, despite his resolve, and now he'd have to deal with the consequences. Like knowing that, instead of making him less distracted, experiencing even a tiny taste of her had all but guaranteed he'd never get her out of his head.

Which wasn't helpful at present. With a gravely injured patient, Jake needed all his wits about him.

He made a pit stop at Wendy's desk on the way to his office. "Any word from CT?"

"Let's see." She clicked a few keys on her computer. "Looks like they're finishing up with your patient as we speak."

"Thanks." Taking the stairs two at a time, he emerged into a bright hallway on the third floor moments later and headed to Radiology.

One of the techs waved Jake into the viewing room, then pointed at her screen. "Doesn't look good, I'm afraid."

She stood, and Jake sank down into her chair, staring at the glowing images. The bullet they'd been searching for was lodged snugly in the patient's brain. Right smack in an area critical for breathing. No amount of trauma surgery would heal that level of damage.

"Can you send these to me?" he asked, his attention frozen on the screen.

"Will do, Dr. Ryder. Sorry the outcome wasn't better."

"Not your fault."

Spirits heavy, Jake called Neurosurgery to have them confirm the dismal prognosis. Two hours later he led the patient's family into a private conference room and told them the heart-wrenching news. Doing his best to keep his emotions out of the equation, Jake answered their questions, deferring to the neurosurgeon when needed, and finally left when there was nothing else to say.

All his training for these scenarios never made them any easier. Bone-deep weariness and a gnawing sense of failure haunted him all the way back to his office. Thankfully his shift was done, because all Jake wanted now was the solitude of his home and his bed. He quietly packed up his stuff and left with only a mumbled farewell to Wendy.

Following a hot shower and a cup of soup for dinner, Jake slipped between his sheets. His eyes felt scratchy from fatigue, but as he drifted off that kid's arrival in the ER replayed in his head. Maybe if he'd done something different, if he'd gotten to the bullet sooner, if…

Slowly the hospital scenes dissolved into his last day in Kandahar…

"Area's secure. No snipers. Nothing suspicious. Ready for transport," Bobby had said as he'd helped clear a space for the helicopters to land safely and retrieve the wounded.

Jake had just finished hooking up an IV when the first bullet had whizzed past him. Next thing he'd known it had been raining ammo like hailstones.

"Get down! Keep the victims covered."

The enemy had seemed to be everywhere—on the roofs, in the walls, behind each corner. Choppers had swooped in and returned fire.

There'd been a village nearby—local civilians who'd been kind to the troops. One house had taken a direct hit, going up in flames while the people inside screamed for help. Without thought Jake had taken off across the battle-field. Behind him Bobby had yelled for him to stop, yelled for his men to provide cover, yelled as three soldiers had crumpled to the ground—dead.

Jake had successfully rescued the trapped family members, after seeing to his own troop's fallen warriors, when white-hot pain had seared up his leg. Dazed, he'd stared down at the wound in his thigh. Must've nicked the femoral artery, he'd thought dazedly, judging by the amount of blood.

It had been as if it was all happening to someone else. Then Bobby had been there, tying a tourniquet, hauling Jake behind a pile of scrap metal, saving his life as agony hacked through Jake like a machete.

"I—I need to h-help them. N-no m-man left b-behind…" Jake's words had trailed off as his world had gone cockeyed. The smell of gunpowder and the salty taste of fear had filled his senses and his consciousness had slipped.

The last thing he remembered was Bobby's words—
"We'll make it, bud!"—and an earsplitting boom.

Eyes snapping open, Jake threw back the bedcovers and
rushed to the bathroom to splash cold water on his face,
swallowing hard against the bile in his throat. He took
deep breaths in and out, in and out, until his thudding pulse
slowed and his mind cleared.

Yeah. Maybe being by himself right now wasn't the best
idea after all.

By the time he made it back to the bedroom and checked
the time it was nearly 5:30 p.m. With his odd schedule he'd
learned to catch a snooze whenever he could, but he'd not
expected to sleep away most of the day. He sank down onto
the edge of the mattress and rubbed his eyes. His favorite
local pub would be open. He could grab a real dinner, have
a drink. Be around people, life, laughter.

Decision made, he pulled on some clothes, then headed
out.

The Snaggle Tooth Pub had always been his and Bobby's go-to hangout. People greeted him as he passed, no one
commenting on his messy hair or haunted eyes.

"What can I get you, Doc?" the bartender asked as Jake
took a seat on one of the stools.

"Pale ale, please."

"Sure thing." The guy returned with an icy bottle of cold
brew and a menu.

Drink in hand, Jake swiveled to survey the room—
cheesy retro décor and moose antlers covered the walls,
and the tang of whiskey and greasy bar food filled the air.
This pub had the best salmon nachos in town. He ordered a
plate from a passing waitress, then took a long swig of his
beer, feeling some of his tension abate.

Then the bell above the door jangled and in walked
Molly. Jake swiveled away quickly, but not before he'd
caught her eye. Images of their heated kiss swarmed in his
overtaxed mind and his body responded before he could stop

it. How had she heard about this place? Was she meeting someone here? It would be better if she was. Not because he didn't enjoy her company, but because he was coming to enjoy it more than he should.

"Is this seat taken?"

Molly's cheerful tone washed over him. He closed his eyes, knowing he should tell her yes even as he shook his head no and hazarded a quick side glance at her. Damn if she didn't look adorable, in jeans and sneakers and some silly green sweatshirt with the symbol for Pi on it, surrounded by the words "Too much gives you a large circumference".

Jake took another swallow of ale, feeling the alcohol swirling through his empty stomach and creating a nice buzz. In fact Molly looked almost as cute tonight as she had in those yoga pants in the workout room. Or in scrubs. Or that T-shirt that first night. Honestly, the woman would look gorgeous in anything.

Or nothing at all…

Jake coughed to clear the sudden constriction in his throat.

She ordered a glass of white wine instead of the frou-frou drink he'd expected. Kellie had always gone for those ridiculous glasses of fruit juice and fairy dust.

Molly's light touch on his forearm made the whole right side of his body tingle.

"I heard about your gunshot patient. I'm sorry."

"Thanks." The word emerged as more of a grunt.

"Bobby's doing okay, though," Molly continued, filling in for his silence. "I checked on him again before I left." She met his gaze, held it before looking away. "You were right."

"Excuse me?"

She frowned—something she always did when she was thinking. "About too much work making me a dull person. Did you know a new study shows a significant difference between being engaged in a task and being addicted to it?"

Yep. There went her brain again. He'd worked with a few

guys like her in the military. Brilliant at what they did, but no social skills at all.

"You're saying I'm compulsive?" Jake took another sip of ale, realized he'd drained the bottle. "I'm the best at what I do."

"So am I." She toyed with the stem of her glass.

He couldn't help wondering how those graceful fingers would feel against his chest, his abs, lower still…

"I have a question for you. More of a proposition."

Her voice cracked a little and he felt the vibration clear to his toes.

Stick around, Bolt. I might have a proposition for you too.

Jake stared at the sticky bar top. That was the alcohol talking—loosening his inhibitions, pushing him to do and say things that were not in his best interest. Apparently one ale was more than enough for him tonight.

He flagged down the bartender. "Can I get a cup of coffee, please?"

"Sure thing." The guy grabbed a steaming pot and returned with a white ceramic mug.

"Anything for you, ma'am?"

"No, thanks," Molly said.

"Great. Your nachos should be out in a minute, Doc."

Once they were alone again, Jake stirred cream and sugar into his coffee, ignoring the burning weight of her stare.

"Will you take me to Dr. Dave's party?" Her question rushed out in a nervous tumble.

Jake froze. "What? Like a date?"

"No." Molly shook her head, sending a few tendrils of hair from her ponytail bobbing around her face.

He longed to reach out and run his fingers through them, but resisted.

"Not a date. More for protection."

"Protection?" He scrunched his nose. "Someone's put a hit out on you already, Bolt?"

She gave him a look. "No. My father will be there. I'd rather not face him alone."

Was it his imagination or were her hands trembling?

All his defending instincts roared into life. As a department head, he'd been invited to the dinner party Dr. Dave had announced he was throwing for Molly's father. Having a professional companion along would make things easier for them both. Still, he wanted to make sure he understood her reasoning.

"Why me? Why not take one of your crew?"

"Rob and Neal are busy with production. I already checked."

"Oh." He took a sip of his coffee. "You really don't like your father, do you?"

"Things between us are…strained."

Finally, he said, "Well, I suppose we could go together—as colleagues."

"Yes. Colleagues. That'd be great."

They sat there for a while, the silence between them growing heavier by the second.

"So, you and Bobby…" she said finally. "How did you guys become friends?"

Jake chuckled, staring down into his coffee. "We met in BCT—basic combat training at Fort Benning, Georgia. He and I went in as officers, because of our college degrees, but that didn't save us from eight and a half weeks of hell. In fact, I think it made it worse, because they were harder on us." Jake snorted. "Anyway, Bobby and I hit it off the first day. We had a lot in common, even though I was from Alaska and he was from the Midwest. My dad was a veteran—so was his. I was an only child—so was he. We both loved hockey and hated clowns."

"Sounds like a match made in heaven."

"Or hell! Bobby eventually had to drop out of Ranger School because of an inner ear problem. He went into the security forces and led the troop that traveled with my regiment. Trouble had a way of following him around even back then. Bobby loved playing practical jokes, and he thought it would be funny to pull a prank on our drill sergeant."

"Is that a good idea?"

"No."

"Yikes."

"Yeah. Of course I was such a cocky idiot that I went right along with his plan. In hindsight…? Big mistake."

"Uh-oh. What happened?" Molly sipped her white wine, her eyes adorably wide.

"We got drunk on leave, then snuck onto base and broke into the sergeant's barracks to booby-trap the shower. The guy was a huge Toronto Blue Jays baseball fan, so we filled the shower head with neon blue dye. When he turned it on it left him looking like a giant Smurf."

"Oh, no!" Molly tried to bite back her giggles and failed. "I'm sorry. That shouldn't be funny, but it is."

"Yeah. We felt pretty proud of ourselves—until the next day at roll call."

"Was your punishment awful?"

"In the long run, not so much. Half a day in the major general's office getting screamed at and a permanent warning in our files. But it sealed the friendship for Bobby and me. Later, on the battlefield—" He stopped himself, not ready to go further quite yet, after his awful day and the nightmare earlier. "Well, we stayed close over the years."

"That's great."

The hint of sadness in Molly's tone had Jake focusing on her again.

"All right. I've told you about me and Bobby. How about you share more about this scary father of yours? You said everything when you were a kid was performance-based. What exactly does that mean?"

She gave a small shrug. "If you didn't meet my father's standards you didn't exist."

"That can't be right."

"No, it's not right. But it's true." Molly sighed. "He was gone a lot with his work—which was good. Because when he was home he'd trot me out to show off for his friends. It was bittersweet, because those were really the only times I spent with him. I hated performing—hated all those people staring at me, judging me. But I did it because it meant I'd have my father's undivided attention and affection for those few precious seconds, even if it was all for show. Back then, I thought if I could prove to him that I was good enough, smart enough, he'd love me."

"My God…" Jake whispered, reaching for her hand.

She let him take it, blinking hard. "It wasn't that bad, really. I had food, clothes, a pretty house…any toys or books I wanted. Nothing to complain about."

"Except love?"

"Except that."

"Wow."

Jake gazed around the bar, trying to figure out the most diplomatic way to ask what he wanted to. In the end he just said it, because he didn't know how else to phrase it. "Why TV, though? I mean, for a person who hates being the center of attention it seems like an odd career move."

She stared into the distance, as if deep in thought. "Originally I started the show as a means to prove to my father that I wasn't the failure he imagined. Then later, once Neal and Rob became my friends, it meant more. I truly do enjoy my cases, even if the travel and filming portions aren't my favorite. And I trust my colleagues to portray me in the best light." She lifted one shoulder and looked back at him. "Does that make sense?"

"It does."

The bartender brought a heaping portion of food and two plates.

Jake set one in front of Molly. "Would you like some? Best salmon nachos in Alaska."

"Oh…um…" She stared at the platter, her stomach growling. "They do smell incredible."

"They're fantastic."

Jake dished some up for her before digging into his own portion. The creamy cheese and salty chips went perfectly with the sweetness of the fish and the spice of the jalapenos.

"What do you think?"

"Really delicious."

Molly licked her lips, and all Jake could think about was kissing her again.

Luckily, she raised her wineglass and held his gaze, a question lurking in her eyes. "To colleagues?"

Her words echoed in his head.

I trust my colleagues…

The significance wasn't lost on him, and nor was the fact that her asking him to Dr. Dave's dinner party was a big deal—another step forward in their relationship. Jake hesitated only slightly before clinking his coffee cup against Molly's wineglass, not missing the slight flicker of guarded joy in her eyes or the matching twinge of hope deep in his chest.

"To colleagues."

CHAPTER SEVEN

"Do I LOOK all right?" Molly asked Jake.

Two days had passed since that night at the bar, and now they were poised before the beautiful carved front door of Dr. Dave's mansion, perched on a hillside of Anchorage's posh neighborhood of Coral Lane. The place was as large as her parents' estate in Oakbrook, though this house seemed much more inviting—at least until she remembered that her father lurked somewhere inside.

The same pulse-pounding fear of rejection and the sickening doubt she always felt in her father's presence welled inside her before she could stop it, choking her breath and making her palms slick. Molly was an accomplished physician in her own right, yet all it took was one pending encounter with her bully of a father to send her right back to the darkest, loneliest days of her childhood.

She smoothed her trembling hand down the front of her little black dress and prayed she looked sophisticated enough—the outfit was the only somewhat formal thing she'd brought. Jake looked marvelous in a suit, the scruff on his jaw adding a mysterious, wild edge. Seeing him out of his scrubs, dapper as Cary Grant in An Affair to Remember, did crazy things to Molly's already overloaded nervous system. So she tried not to look at him often. And failed. Miserably.

"You look beautiful," Jake said, his voice low and sincere.

Her stomach fluttered anew, this time from pure sweetness. Still, Molly had to be rational. This was a business arrangement. Strictly platonic. An evening between colleagues despite that soul-searing kiss they'd shared in the gym. Besides, getting involved with a man who lived half a world away would never work out. It would be foolish.

Too bad none of that seemed to matter a bit to her yearning heart.

Time to take the plunge.

Raising her shaky hand, Molly rang the bell. "Here goes nothing."

"You got this, Bolt." Jake gave her a little nudge with his shoulder and the shadows closing in on her seemed to recede slightly.

A stunning older woman with dark hair and a model-perfect figure, answered the door. "Hello," she said, her smile broad. "Always a pleasure to see you, Jake."

They embraced. Jake kissed the woman on the cheek, then placed a gentle hand on Molly's lower back, playing the part of doting date extremely well. So well, in fact, that if Molly wasn't careful she'd forget all this was pretend.

"And you must be Dr. Flynn." The woman extended a hand to Molly. "I'm Sara Carpenter—Dave's wife. I love your show, by the way. My favorite was Toe Fungus Guy."

"Thank you. That episode seems to be popular."

Molly stepped inside the house, thankful for the reassuring presence of Jake's hand guiding her forward. Sara took Molly's coat and hung it in a nearby closet, then led them down a short hall toward the sounds of a party in full swing.

The home was a perfect combination of rustic charm and modern convenience—an Alpine cathedral, with walls and floors made entirely of caramel-colored pine and ceilings soaring at least twenty-five feet above them. Oriental carpets and dark leather furniture helped make the huge open spaces seem homier. At one end of a spacious great room sat a giant stone fireplace, flames crackling merrily inside.

Molly felt thoroughly charmed—until she spotted her father, standing to one side of the room, deep in conversation with Dr. Dave. The sound of her pounding heart thudded loud in her ears, drowning out everything else.

Hands clenched tight at her sides, Molly did her best to maintain a cool façade while hoping to avoid her father for as long as possible. With a polite smile, she turned to her hostess. "Your home is spectacular. I'd love to see the rest."

"Absolutely." Sara gestured toward the nearby hallway. "I adore giving tours."

"Since I've been here a million times, I'll just head over and chat with the other department heads," Jake said, backing away slowly. "Unless you need me, Molly?"

Though every fiber of her being screamed for her to keep him close by her side all night, she knew deep down that she needed to face this on her own. Besides, given the way her father had ripped Brian to shreds on a regular basis, Molly didn't want Jake to face the same fate.

She forced words out. "No. That's fine. I'll see you in a few minutes."

Molly followed Sara out of the great room and into a grand chef's kitchen, full of stainless steel appliances and granite countertops. "Wow!"

"Yes, it's a bit breathtaking, isn't it? We hadn't planned on going quite so overboard when we built the place, but Dave and I figured this is it. Might as well get what we want, right?"

"It's amazing."

Molly ran her fingertips along the edge of a counter, wishing she could lay her heated cheek against the cool stone for a while. A familiar buzzing had started inside her head and her dread grew. Random facts and inappropriate responses zinged like pinballs through her mind.

Please don't let me embarrass myself—not now.

"Martha would have an orgasm and die in here," Molly said, unable to stop herself.

Too late.

"I'm so sorry. I didn't mean that the way it sounded." Fresh heat prickled Molly's cheeks. "What I meant was my sister loves to cook and would really enjoy such a well-appointed kitchen."

"I understand." Sara burst out laughing. "As a fellow foodie, rest assured I had the same reaction my first time too. I think you and I will get along just fine."

Molly smiled back, her usual awkwardness disappearing with Sara's genuine friendliness. "I hope so. I tend to rub people up the wrong way sometimes."

"Really? Why?"

"When I get overly stressed or nervous I recite odd random facts." Just one more thing her father had made her feel bad about. "Or I say snarky, strange things."

"Well, I admire people who speak their minds—if it's done with kindness. And I'm sure your facts are fascinating. I can't imagine how a brilliant mind like yours works." Sara linked arms with Molly. "Come on. I'll show you the rest of the place."

They viewed several bedrooms and a master bathroom larger than Molly's entire apartment in Chicago. By the time the tour ended they were upstairs in a loft, overlooking the first level, and Molly felt almost calm again. From all the way up here her father appeared a bit less intimidating. But only a little.

Molly shuddered and refocused her attention elsewhere. In the crowd below Jake was working the room like a pro, shaking hands and laughing. He seemed so attentive, so genuinely interested in everyone in his life.

What she wouldn't give to have him feel that way about her too. Not that she was in his life, exactly—not permanently anyway. A pang of sadness ached inside her—which was absurd. They'd shared one kiss.

A heart-melting, steamy kiss…

As if sensing her gaze, Jake glanced up at Molly and waved, his crooked grin making her knees tingle. She waved back, sending him a goofy grin of her own.

"Are you married?" Sara asked.

"No." Molly gripped the thick wooden banister, wishing it was Jake's arm instead. Amazing how fast she'd come to rely on his support. "Recently single, actually."

"Hmm…" Sara pushed away from the railing and started downstairs. "C'mon. Let's get you something to drink before you see your father. He's been asking about you."

They returned to the kitchen and Molly chose a glass of Cabernet.

"Must be hard," Sara said, pouring a generous serving for Molly then recorking the bottle, her expression thoughtful.

"I'm sorry?" Molly sipped the rich wine. She'd not eaten since breakfast, and the next few hours would be difficult enough without getting tipsy. Not to mention she was on call for Bobby and having trouble controlling her reactions to Jake. No need to loosen those inhibitions any more.

"Having the illustrious Roger Flynn as your dad," Sara said. "That must be very hard."

Molly stared out through the expanse of window across from her. Streaks of gold, purple and indigo colored the expansive Alaskan sunset. She'd love to lie and say she'd learned so much from her brilliant father, that he'd supported her in her life and her career. That he hadn't reduced her self-confidence to zilch and then blamed her for being too shy and having no friends.

Instead, she said nothing at all. Just gave a sad little shrug.

"Ah!" Dr. Dave walked into the kitchen, shattering the silence and making Molly jump. "I wondered what had happened to you ladies."

"I taught you better than to skulk in corners, daughter of mine."

Roger Flynn strolled into the room, and Molly's oxygen seemed to evaporate. He looked the same as always—designer suit, perfectly styled silver hair, icy green eyes. Intimidating. Imposing. He gave Molly a quick air-kiss, not touching her, and her face ached from the strain of keeping her smile in place. In his assessing gaze, she saw judgment and disappointment. Par for the course.

"When do we eat?" Dr. Dave asked, oblivious to the electric tension in the air. "Molly, Orion's Catering makes the best pot roast this side of the Rockies. You're in for a treat."

She tore her attention away from her father's disapproving stare to focus on their charming hosts. Had her parents ever been that happy? Her stomach churned—not from hunger but from anxiety. Molly could barely remember her parents holding hands, let alone being affectionate with each other.

She swallowed hard around the lump of sadness in her throat. "It smells wonderful, Dr. Dave."

"Hey, Sara. Got any pale ale?" Jake strolled in, his gaze resting on Molly as he stepped closer to her side, his arm brushing hers as he whispered, "Everything okay, Bolt?"

The endearment reminded Molly of their heated kiss and warmed her from the inside out—not enough to thaw the frigid ice caused by her father's looming presence, but a start.

Craving his support, she pressed closer, aware of her father watching their every move. "Everything's fine, thank you, Dr. Ryder."

At Molly's use of his professional title, Jake cocked a brow.

"Jake, have you met our guest of honor?" Dr. Dave said congenially. "Dr. Jake Ryder—may I introduce Dr. Roger Flynn?"

The two men shook hands briskly, silently assessing each other in a blatant display of masculine bravado Molly had seen too many times to count around her father. It was like Wild Kingdom—except in place of the bull elephants or stallions there were alpha surgeons.

"Pleasure," Jake said.

"I'm sure." Roger Flynn knocked back the rest of his liquor, and regarded his younger rival with cool interest.

"Dr. Ryder's my Head of Emergency Medicine," Dr. Dave said with pride. "Finest trauma surgeon in the state of Alaska."

"Rather a tiny pond of comparison, isn't it?" her father said under his breath.

Jake's posture stiffened. "We're the largest level one trauma center in the region."

"Ryder cut his teeth in combat. Courage under fire," Dr. Dave continued on affably, as if a professional gauntlet hadn't been thrown down.

Molly was torn between wanting to see her father flayed alive for his insults and wanting to protect Jake from the man's cruelty.

"You both have that in common. The love of adventure, the thrill of danger—"

"Here you go." Sara passed Jake a bottle of ale, then gave her husband a Be quiet look. "Dinner will be ready shortly. Why don't you all go mingle?"

"Dr. Ryder," her father said, with all the friendliness of a frozen cod.

Once he'd left Molly exhaled and placed her glass on the center island. "I'm so sorry."

"About what?" Jake looked perplexed.

"About my father's behavior." She shook her head. "I'm glad he left before things got worse."

Jake still hadn't moved from her side, and he stared after her father. "He's…interesting. And pompous. But I saw far worse displays from the five-star generals and Pentagon big-wigs in Afghanistan. You want to talk egos? Go a couple rounds with those guys."

"Really?" Molly's breath hitched and the large kitchen seemed to close in on her. Oh, God. Not a panic attack, please. She squeezed her eyes shut. "You okay, Bolt?" Jake rubbed her back and leaned closer. "Is there anything I can do?"

"F-fresh air," she managed to gasp.

"Right. Excuse us," he said to their hosts, who had already moved toward the door, and then he slipped his arm around her waist and pulled her into his side. "I've got you."

Molly clung to him, appreciating his quiet strength and confidence. Brian had always mocked her panic attacks, claiming she only did it to get attention. Her father had always simply ignored them, considering them another unfortunate sign of Molly's weakness. Jake, however, didn't bat an eye, shielding her from the curious stares of the other guests as he guided her toward a secluded space off the main great room.

Gradually the pressure in Molly's chest eased and she sucked in a much-needed breath. A shiver ran through her and Jake held her tighter, his gray gaze concerned.

"We're almost there, sweetheart. Hang on for me, okay?"

"Okay." Molly gave him a small smile, her heart aching at the endearment. "Thank you."

"For what?"

"For being so nice to me. I'm not used to being coddled."

Jake got Molly settled on the window seat then crouched in front of her, lacing her icy fingers with his, stroking idle circles over her palm with his thumb, soft and infinitely tender. "After meeting your father, I'm not surprised. But we're in this together, right?"

"Yes."

His steady caress and the lulling deepness of his voice had her hypnotized. Molly leaned closer…so close she could kiss him again…

"Bolt?" he said, his voice huskier. "Do I need to take you into my ER?"

The mention of the hospital broke through Molly's haze at last and she blinked hard to clear her fuzzy head. It wasn't the wine. She'd only had a couple of sips. But Jake was proving to be more intoxicating than any alcohol.

"No," she managed to say at last.

Her hand was braced against his chest, feeling the thud

of his heart beating in time with hers. She took another deep breath and the room around her expanded again, filling with the low hum of chatter.

She smoothed Jake's lapel and gave him a shaky smile. "I'm better. Thank you."

"Good." He grasped her chin between his thumb and forefinger and grinned. "Now, quit thanking me. You can make it up to me later, Bolt."

Jake took a seat beside Molly, his shoulder resting comfortably against hers. She had no idea how to repay him for such kindness, but the possibilities caused all sorts of naughty butterflies to shiver through her stomach.

"Dinner is served," Sara said from near the grand fireplace. "Please, come into the dining room and find your assigned seats."

Food was the last thing on Molly's mind, but thankfully Jake stayed steadfastly by her side at the table. Catering staff bustled around, filling water goblets and placing plates before each guest.

Molly took a tentative bite of the tangy arugula and tomato salad with a balsamic vinaigrette dressing as her father regarded her with cool assessment from across the table.

"Tell me about your latest case," Roger Flynn said.

After a quick glance at Jake, Molly relayed the medical details about Bobby while keeping his identity secret. "We're following a conservative approach to allow the patient's system time to recover."

"Conservative only produces mediocre results." Her father scoffed. "Where's your ingenuity?"

"Ingenuity isn't always what's needed in an acute situation," Jake intervened, his tone icy. "As I'm sure you understand."

"Ingenuity is what creates medical breakthroughs," her father said, his tone seething. "I would've expected more bravery from a combat veteran."

Jake tensed. "On the battlefield, my number one priority was to get the wounded triaged as quickly and safely as possible. Not to chase the next big innovation."

"Innovation saves lives." Her father's green eyes had frozen like Siberian emeralds. "Without pushing the boundaries, we never know how far we can go."

"I was raised to respect boundaries."

"More's the pity." Her father gave a dismissive snort. "Boundaries are your downfall."

"And your ego is yours." Jake glared at Roger Flynn, a muscle ticking near his tense jaw. "You don't have any compassion for anyone, do you?"

"I'm the top trauma surgeon in the world, Dr. Ryder. Compassion is a luxury I can't afford. In my world respect must be earned—as my daughter can attest."

Molly's heart plummeted. She could attest all too well to his stringent demands and lofty ideals, which she had never attained. She'd failed him again and again, always falling short of his impossibly high standards, of his dreams for what he'd wanted in a daughter. As an adult, she should be past caring, but it still stung.

Beneath the table, Jake took her hand. Molly hazarded a glance over at him, expecting to see a defeated man, scraped raw from her father's scathing insults. Instead Jake gave her a small half-grin and squeezed her fingers tight.

Confused, she started to whisper, "I'm—"

"I'm going to start keeping count of those apologies, Bolt. A few more and before long you're going to owe me more than you can ever repay." His grin widened. "Now, eat up."

Stunned, Molly continued to nibble on her salad. Brian had always cowered before her father's bully tactics. But Jake? Well, he hadn't backed down an inch. He'd defended her.

No one had ever chosen Molly's side before.

The waiter removed their salad plates and replaced them with heaping portions of pot roast and grilled vegetables. The delicious sweet smell of tomatoes and carrots mixed with the rich aroma of braised beef had Molly's appetite returning.

She was about to dig in when her phone buzzed from inside her evening bag and her pulse tripped. She was expecting lab results on Bobby.

"Excuse me a moment."

Molly walked back into the living room, pulling out her phone and hitting redial as she wandered toward the windows. In the valley below the lights of Anchorage sparkled like diamonds, and she could almost picture herself building a new life in this rugged place…raising a family, making a real home here with Jake…

A technician answered, putting an abrupt end to her daydreams.

"Lab."

"Yes, this is Dr. Flynn. I got a message that my patient's results are in."

"Yes. Hang on a moment, please."

"What's going on?"

Jake came up behind her, the heat of him surrounding her. She held up a finger as the technician returned to the line.

"Dr. Flynn, Bobby Templeton's BUN and creatinine levels are rising. You said to call with any changes."

"Yes. Thank you." She ended the call, then dialed Gladys's extension. "How's Bobby?" she asked.

As Molly waited for the nurse to pull his records she turned to Jake.

"Hospital calling with results."

"Any change?"

Gladys came back on the line. "Mr. Templeton's lung function is deteriorating, his fever's back, and that rash on his legs is spreading to his torso."

"Damn," Molly said.

"What?" Jake moved closer, his hand returning to her lower back.

She rubbed her temple as she relayed to him what she'd found out. "I'm afraid your treatment plan isn't working."

Roger Flynn had walked into the room as well, and was giving them both a disparaging stare. "I told you. Conservative methods won't yield—"

"Please, shut up!" Molly said before she could stop herself.

Eyes wide, she snapped her mouth closed. Before tonight she'd never had the gumption to talk back to her father. Perhaps Jake's attitude was rubbing off.

"How dare you—?"

"The lady said shut up!" Jake growled, cutting her father off again.

Molly finished with Gladys, then faced Jake. "What's your diagnosis?"

"Metabolic disorder?"

Jake looked as agitated as she felt, but Dr. Dave had been right. They did work better as a team. The rest of the room disappeared as they brainstormed ideas.

"Something genetic—mitochondrial, maybe?"

"Perhaps we should try my protocol? The hyperbaric chamber would force more oxygen into his blood, helping him to heal faster."

"No. I'm sorry, Bolt, but I stand by my decision. We need to avoid any treatments that could put Bobby's future career as an athlete at risk. Nothing wacky."

"Wacky?" After dealing with her father tonight, the word hit a bit too close to all the old insults that had been hurled her way as a kid.

"She's very smart, but a bit of a wacky mess when it comes to her social skills," her father had used to joke to his colleagues.

She stepped away from Jake, frowning. "There's nothing wrong with using a hyperbaric chamber."

"It's a bit unorthodox—even you admit that. I prefer the tried and true."

He reached for her hand again, his expression imploring, but she pulled away.

Jake's smile fell. "C'mon, Molly. I've seen your show. 'Unorthodox' doesn't begin to cover your treatment methods. If I allowed you free rein we'd have Bobby strung up by his toes with a voodoo priestess dancing around his room."

Snickers rang out around the room—including from her father.

Gone was the warm, fuzzy comfort she'd felt with Jake earlier. Now Molly felt only exposed, raw to the bone—the same way she had during those dreaded performances for her father as a child.

She stalked away from Jake, with her father's vexed glare forever burning in her mind. Coming here tonight had been a mistake. Inviting Jake as her date had been even worse. She'd opened up to him, let him see her most vulnerable side—had begun to think of him as her partner in this case, maybe more. She'd thought he was different...that maybe he might see past her flaws and care for her anyway.

But she'd been wrong.

Eyes stinging, Molly rushed toward the foyer. All she wanted to do was get back to Anchorage Mercy—back to her comfort zone, back to the one place where she felt competent and successful.

Ignoring the inquiring looks of the other guests, who'd filed into the living room to see what all the commotion was about, Molly yanked her coat from the closet. "Thank you for the lovely dinner, Dr. Dave... Sara. I'm going back to the hospital to take care of my patient. I'll do my best not to try anything wacky while you're gone, Dr. Ryder."

Jake made his own quick farewells, then stormed after Molly toward her Range Rover. "Mind telling me what just happened?"

"Yes, actually." The lights on the vehicle flickered as she jabbed a button on her key fob. "I do."

Pulling open the passenger side door, Jake climbed into the seat, barely managing to get the door closed again before Molly revved the engine and took off down the long, winding driveway. He'd been in bombing raids friendlier than the vibe he was getting from her at this point—though her stress was understandable. Her father was a complete ass.

Still, Jake thought they'd handled things well tonight. He'd had her back—would've protected Molly against Roger Flynn or any other blowhard in that room. Bobby's case had brought them together, but tonight had made them a team. At least that was how he'd felt. He'd even found himself, against all odds, trusting her. More than he had anyone else in a long time.

The tension around her mouth now and the paleness of her cheeks bothered him, though. Hoping to regain some solidarity, he said, "Boy, your dad's a piece of work."

Molly swerved out onto the main road, tires squealing. "I don't want to discuss him."

"Pull over and let me drive." Jake gripped the dashboard as she passed another vehicle, switching lanes without signaling. "Please."

"What's the matter?" Molly glanced over at him and ran up onto the berm, bumping noisily before she merged onto the Seward Highway heading toward Anchorage Mercy, a wild spark in her eyes. "Afraid I'll go all wacky on you?"

"If this vehicle being wrapped around a utility pole is your idea of wacky, then, yeah."

"My driving skills are exemplary, thank you very much." Molly gripped the wheel tight, her fingers tapping out a rapid cadence. "Many more men than women die each year in motor vehicle crashes. Men typically drive more miles and engage in more risky driving practices, including not using safety belts and operating a vehicle while intoxicated."

"Speaking of alcohol—how much wine did you have?"

"A few sips." She gave him a withering stare. "But don't you prefer girls who drink pale ale?"

He sat back, exasperated. "Since when do you care what kinds of girls I prefer?"

"I didn't say I cared. I just—"

"What? Feel like prying into my private life?" Furious, he turned away. "Typical media."

"And we're rehashing that again." Molly jammed on the brakes as they approached a red light, screeching to an undignified halt. "Is that all you've got? Boo-hoo. The big, bad media's out to get me."

"You're one to talk. What was all that kowtowing to your dad in there, huh? What are you? His slave? No, wait. His irritatingly intelligent fact-spouter? Does he rent you out for parties?"

The angry flush in Molly's cheeks drained away and she lowered her gaze, her stiff posture slumping.

Remorse clunked heavily in Jake's chest. He'd gone too far. But damn if she hadn't pushed all his buttons. Part of him wanted to get out of the vehicle and call a taxi. The other part of him wanted to pull Molly into his lap and kiss her until they both forgot about this disaster of a night— forgot about everything except the incredible chemistry between them.

The car behind them honked. The light had turned green.

Molly accelerated—slower this time. They traveled on in silence for several minutes, until she said quietly, "Why don't you like the media? The truth."

He sighed. "I received an honorable discharge in August 2011. The following February they awarded me and Bobby Distinguished Service Crosses for extraordinary heroism on the battlefield in Kandahar. With the stress of trying to assimilate back into civilian life with my ex and my new job at Anchorage Mercy, the added pressure the media put on our relationship was the final straw. The fact Kellie was infatuated with all the attention didn't help. Between my need for privacy and her need for the spotlight, it finally tore us apart."

"Oh." She looked at him, her eyes sad in the greenish glow of the dashboard. "I'm sorry."

"Didn't we agree you wouldn't say that anymore, Bolt?" He flashed her a half-hearted smile, then stared out his window at the lights of his Alaskan hometown. "Anyway, by the end I'd become isolated, and protective of my privacy. Kellie blamed me for all her problems and said I was holding her back. She ended up moving to New York for some big network job without even discussing it with me. The press had a field-day with that too, by the way. And I was totally blindsided by Kellie leaving. I'd trusted her. I'd thought the war had done a number on me, but I was wrong. Kellie's betrayal and those reporters screwed me up a hell of a lot worse."

"Yes, I can understand your resentment now." Molly concentrated on the road ahead, her expression contemplative.

"Tell me why you let your father treat you the way he does," he said, turning the tables.

"That's the way it's always been."

"Doesn't make it right."

"No." She shrugged. "But it makes things easier. His bullying only gets worse if I fight back or try to defend myself. I'm different than the rest of my family."

"How so?"

"Well, let's see… My mother is a socialite extraordinaire. My older sister is a junior Martha Stewart on steroids. And you've just experienced Superstar Roger Flynn, able to do amazing feats of surgery with a single bound."

"What about you?"

"What about me?"

"What's your special power? Besides the whole genius thing."

"That's pretty much all I've got." Molly gave a sad little snort. "That's why I'm such a big disappointment. I'm not beautiful. I'm hopeless in social situations. And I'm definitely not the kind of daughter Roger Flynn thinks he deserves. But my intellect's given me many opportunities, so I can't complain."

"Sure you can." Jake swallowed hard against the lump of remorse in his throat. "And I'm sorry for calling your methods wacky back there. I understand now why that touched a nerve."

She acknowledged his apology with a single nod.

The tension in the air lifted and Jake couldn't resist stealing another glance at her. It astonished him that Molly thought she wasn't beautiful. She was quite possible the most exquisite thing he'd ever seen.

At last they turned in to the Anchorage Mercy parking lot and Molly pulled up beside Jake's truck. They walked inside the hospital, heading for the elevators.

Molly punched the buttons, then took out her phone, frowning. "Is Bobby a heavy drinker or involved in any illicit drug use?"

"No. He's the biggest health nut I've ever met. You read the list of his supplements, right?"

"I did…"

The elevator dinged and they stepped onboard. Jake leaned a shoulder against the wall while Molly scrolled through the texts on her phone screen.

"None of them explain all his symptoms, though."

Dread pooled thick and heavy in his gut. "We have to do something. I can't lose him. He saved my life back in the desert. That's why he got his commendation."

They arrived on the fourth floor and walked over to Gladys's desk.

"Any more changes since we talked?" Molly asked.

"How was the party?" Rob said, coming down the hall toward them, Neal by his side. "Any juicy tidbits?"

Molly shook her head, casting Jake a quick glance before answering. "Nope."

"Too bad," Neal said. "Network says we need more sizzle."

"This is a medical show, not TMZ." Molly pushed past her crew and grabbed her lab coat.

Jake thought it was a shame she had to cover up the outfit, but he could see how it might be distracting, the way it hugged her curves in all the right places. Then again, he found just about everything about Molly distracting these days.

"Dr. Ryder," she said. "Can I see you in my office a moment, please?"

"Uh…sure." He followed her into the tiny shoebox they'd given her to use.

Molly closed the door and they were alone again. It would be so easy to lean in, to kiss her deeply, to show her she was more than her smarts, more than Diagnosis Critical, more than perfect enough for him.

Molly moved past Jake to grab her stethoscope and it took every shred of his inner strength not to pull her against him. She wore her hair loose tonight, and he remembered the feel of it when she'd leaned against him at Dr. Dave's house, all silky and soft. Making him imagine how he'd like to clutch those thick strands in his hands as he lost himself inside her.

As if sensing the erotic turn of his thoughts, Molly stepped back, her eyes glittering a bit too bright. "I know we agreed I wouldn't, but I want to make one final apology about what happened tonight."

"Accepted." Jake shuffled his feet. "I'm sorry too."

"For what?"

"For your father being a selfish, insufferable bastard."

"Oh, well." She frowned down at the floor. "We Flynns aren't exactly a model family."

He tipped her chin up with his finger. "You deserve better, Molly."

"Um… I've…uh…been thinking about doing some sightseeing while I'm here."

Her voice trailed off, and her cheeks were blazing so red

Jake could practically feel the heat pulsing off them. She tended to ramble when she was nervous or scared. One more endearing thing about his Molly.

His Molly?

His mind snagged on that thought. "I'd be happy to show you around. When's your next day off?"

"Day after tomorrow. I thought I'd book a whale-watching cruise."

"I'm off then too." He smiled. "Let's do it."

She grinned back. "All right."

"All right."

Molly held his gaze for several moments, and the air between them vibrated with delicious possibilities.

She smoothed a hand down the front of her lab coat and gave a slight nod. "Great. Okay. Back to work. We're thinking some type of metabolic disorder?"

It took a second for the abrupt switch in topic to penetrate the fog of desire clouding Jake's brain. "Uh…yeah, I don't see what else it could be, given Bobby's history."

"Right." Molly yanked open the door and walked back to Gladys's desk, where she pushed aside the tray with a small teapot and a mug of brown gunk sitting on the counter and opened the patient's file. "Jake, look at these labs to make sure I'm not missing something."

Forgetting about the cameras rolling, he did as she requested, his nose wrinkling at the foul stench. "Jeez, Gladys. What's that crap you're drinking? Smells like dead rat."

"That's not mine." The nurse grimaced. "It's Bobby's tea. His hockey coach brings him in a batch whenever he visits. Nothing except herbs and water, but it stinks to high heaven."

Molly paused and picked up the mug, sniffing it. "Is there a box this comes in?"

"Yep." Gladys walked over to one of the trash bags awaiting pick-up and pulled out a torn foil packet. "Here."

"Yohimbe." Molly looked from the packet to Jake. "One

of five pausinystalia evergreen species growing in West and Central Africa in lowland forests. The side effects include high blood pressure, increased heart-rate, headache, nausea, tremors and sleeplessness." She turned to Gladys again. "How often has Mr. Templeton been drinking this?"

"Not so much now, but at first he had several cups a day."

Molly faced Jake again, her smile dazzling. "That's it. This works by opening the lungs and increasing blood flow. If Bobby ingested this tea and then received an injection of epinephrine in the ER—"

"It explains his cardiac arrest." Awe and adrenaline rushed Jake's system. "We can take the heart issues out of the equation."

"Yes." Molly's gaze narrowed. "And all the rest of his symptoms point to a long-term severe allergic reaction. Which was the original diagnosis."

"Cut!" Neal said, shutting off the mic. "Perfect, Mol. Nice delivery."

Jake shoved his hands in his pockets. He'd forgotten all about her film crew. Molly did that to him—made him forget about everything but her whenever she was around.

"Don't worry. I'll make sure they edit you out," she said, her eyes never leaving his. "And I'll text you. With the details of the whale cruise?"

"Great." Jake backed away, feeling oddly reluctant to leave.

Molly bit her lower lip. "Goodnight."

"'Night." As he walked away, Jake couldn't remember ever craving a day off more.

CHAPTER EIGHT

BRIGHT AND EARLY Tuesday morning, Molly bounced on the balls of her feet outside the local superstore, waiting to board the bus that would take her and Jake to the Kenai Fjords National Park and their day of whale-watching.

"All right, folks," the driver said from near the door. "Everyone have your vouchers handy and watch your step. Thank you."

The small crowd of about thirty people shuffled forward. Most of them looked to be retirees, though there were a few younger couples with kids and a small quadrant of teens.

"Are you going to be warm enough?" Jake asked, eyeing her new candy-pink outerwear.

The man at the sporting goods store had sworn the high-tech fabric was guaranteed to fifty below zero. She figured the coat, plus her new hat and gloves, would be enough to ward off the chill of any passing glaciers.

Molly gave Jake a quick once-over as they neared the front of the line. He was decked out in sturdy hiking boots and thick plaid shirts doubled up over a taupe thermal Henley. He'd topped it all off with a brown canvas jacket and a black knit skull cap that made him look as if he'd walked straight off the set of Deadliest Catch. Despite his bundled-up appearance, he was still distractingly gorgeous.

"I'll be fine."

Molly handed her excursion ticket to the driver, then climbed up the steps into the bus. Jake followed close behind, once again placing his hand on her lower back to guide her toward a pair of open seats. Even through the extra layers his touch sent sizzles of awareness through her blood.

"This work for you?" He pulled off his hat and shoved

it in his pocket, then ran his hand through his disheveled brown curls.

Molly swallowed hard and looked away. They weren't even out of the parking lot and all she could think about was sliding her hands beneath those thick flannel shirts. "Yes, this is fine."

They sidled into their row and Jake raised the armrest in the middle to give them more room. Comfy as the seats were, Molly couldn't help brushing against him each time she moved, ratcheting her pulse higher as the driver pulled out of the parking lot and their trip got underway.

Exhaling, she focused out the window and struggled to get a grip. Bad enough she'd spent most of the night tossing and turning. After the way things had ended with Brian, Molly didn't want to make the same mistakes with Jake. Nor did she want to go overboard yet, even though she was passionately drawn to him.

"Welcome to Wild Frontier Whale-Watching Excursions," their driver said over the PA system. "We'll be out of Anchorage proper in a few minutes, folks, so settle in and prepare to see the most gorgeous scenery on earth. Have your cameras ready and have a wonderful day!"

"This is probably old hat for you, huh?" Molly said, glancing over at Jake.

"No, actually." He shrugged. "Workaholic, remember? I don't get out here often."

"Right." She watched the urban landscape change to thick green forest. "I was afraid you'd be bored."

"I'm lots of things when I'm with you, Molly, but bored isn't one of them."

His words ignited a fresh burst of excitement inside her.

As they rode along Molly snapped photos of the passing scenery while Jake read the copy of the latest emergency medicine journal he'd brought. About an hour into their trip a tour helper came around with complimentary cups of coffee and pre-packaged pastries.

"I'll pay you back for this," Jake said, unwrapping and devouring half his blueberry muffin in one bite.

"No need." Molly carefully removed her lemon Danish from the cellophane, then unfolded her paper napkin. "Breakfast is included."

"No, I mean the tour." He eyed her neatly prepared area with amusement. "You're tidy too, huh?"

"Is that a problem?"

"No, not a problem."

He gave her a slow appraisal, from the top of her head to the tips of her toes, now curled up inside her hiking boots. His gaze held an answering flicker of heat to match the growing inferno inside her. Her whole body seemed to tremble after his frank perusal.

"But these tours are expensive. I'll pay you back for my share, Molly."

"How about we call this payback for all my nonstop apologies last night?"

Light broke through the hazy clouds gathered near the mountaintops and streamed through the spruce trees, highlighting more of the glorious late fall landscape. Rich scarlets and golds and deep, dark greens hugged the roadway.

Jake chuckled. "Yeah, okay. We can do that."

Molly hazarded another glance at him. "I'm just glad I got you out of the hospital."

"And I'm glad I got you away from your crew for a couple of hours."

"It's nice to have a break."

"It's been so long I've forgotten what it's like to just relax and enjoy a day off." He gave her a sad little half-smile, his tone holding regret mixed with a hint of guilt. "After Kellie left I threw myself into my career, made a lot of sacrifices to get where I am today. Sometimes I wonder if they were worth it—wonder if I'm in control of my career or if it's controlling me."

Without thinking, Molly took his hand. "I think about

those things too. Especially when I see people my age getting married and having kids. My sister's pregnancy hasn't helped. Not that I'm not happy for Martha. I am. I just..." She sighed. "I always wanted children someday."

"Me too." Jake stared down at their entwined fingers. "But we've got plenty of time."

"My mother's fond of reminding how fertility drops off after age thirty."

"I just don't get your family." He frowned. "Both my parents are off traveling the US in their Winnebago, but they're always my biggest supporters. Through school, the military, the end of my engagement to Kellie—everything. Your family doesn't seem to be there for you at all."

"Like I said, I'm the oddball. I don't think they have a clue how to support me, so they just pretend I'm not there." Molly ate the last of her pastry. This was stepping into unknown territory. Brian had never liked to discuss anything unpleasant. "Tell me about your ex-fiancée."

"Kellie and I had known each other since high school. She was a cheerleader and I was on the football team, but we didn't start dating until freshman year of college. She was always volunteering for stuff...trying to get everyone to like her. I pictured us having a white picket fence kind of future."

"Sounds perfect." Molly's heart pinched.

"Obviously not perfect enough." Jake stretched his long legs out in front of him. "Considering she chose her career over me."

The driver's voice crackled over the PA system again. "Folks, if you look toward the right side of the bus you'll see some of the mudflats that make up the Turnagain Pass shoreline."

Molly took a couple more shots while Jake rested his head back against his seat and closed his eyes. She watched him through her lashes, hesitant. Talking about her abysmal break-up with Brian wasn't her favorite topic, but he'd shared about his ex, so it seemed only fair.

"I was seeing someone back in Chicago. His name was Brian."

Jake peeked one eye open and glanced at her, but didn't say anything.

"He was a stockbroker. Smart, educated, looked good on paper. In reality…? Not so much. At least not for me." Molly stared out at Cook Inlet. "Guess I wasn't the person he expected me to be. Story of my life." Her eyes stung again. "He broke up with me. By text message." She shook her head. "How pathetic does that make me?"

Jake gave her fingers a reassuring squeeze. "He's the pathetic one—not you."

"My family might say otherwise."

"The more I learn about your family, the more I'm starting to believe they're a bunch of idiots."

The conviction in his tone, coupled with the spark of understanding in his eyes, had Molly wanting to melt into a puddle of goo at his feet.

Jake smiled. "You're just…different."

"And if that isn't a nice way of saying weird, I don't know what is."

"Hey, I happen to like weird."

"You do?"

"Yeah…" He tugged her closer. "I do."

Molly snuggled into Jake's side and he slipped his arm around her shoulders, guiding her head down to rest on his chest. She did her best not to swoon while he stroked her hair.

"Tell me more about what it was like for you growing up," he said, his voice rumbling comfortingly beneath her ear.

"Being gifted isn't all it's cracked up to be." Molly started to pull away, but Jake held her in place until she relaxed once more. "My parents meant well, I suppose—always pushing, always demanding more, always criticizing—but I felt incredible pressure to achieve, to earn their love and respect. In a lot of ways I still do." She swallowed hard. "Sounds silly."

"Not silly at all. Justified." Jake massaged the nape of her neck, his voice both firm and protective. "Like I said, Molly. You deserved better. You deserve better now."

Hearing him defend her so ardently rekindled that deep yearning inside her. Maybe getting closer to him, if only for a little while, wasn't such an impossibility after all. "Okay..."

"Okay." He leaned past her to point toward the window. "Look. Sea lions."

Resisting the urge to close the tiny gap between them and kiss his cheek, Molly gazed out at the colony basking in the sun on the mudflats. "Cute!"

"Yeah. Adorable..."

Except Jake was looking at her, not the view.

"Welcome aboard the scenic wildlife cruise portion of your trip through the Kenai Fjords. My name's Captain Fred and this is my assistant Joe. We'll be here to point out interesting sights and to answer any questions you may have. Enjoy your day!"

The gruff-looking older man headed back into the ship's cabin to steer them out into the open waters.

Jake leaned against the rail beside Molly, feeling lighter than he had in years. He didn't share his past with many people, but with her it had felt right. He gripped the railing, his hands itching to touch her, stroke her, gather her close and hold her tight.

He stared out at the placid blue water, releasing the stress of the past few days. He'd had precious little respect for Roger Flynn before that dinner party, and after hearing Molly talk about her painful childhood he liked the guy even less. Her father might be brilliant in his chosen field, but his life outside of trauma surgery left a lot to be desired.

The irony wasn't lost on Jake.

If he wasn't careful he could end up heading down that same lonely path.

Several tourists nearby gasped as two dorsal fins slipped through the water about two hundred feet away—orcas, most likely. Jake pointed them out to Molly, but he much preferred to look at her. The wind had flushed her cheeks a delightful shade of pink. Her lips were parted. He wondered what would happen if he leaned in and kissed her again. Would she want more or push him away?

Jake cleared his throat and battled the erotic images flooding his mind, croaking out the first dumb thing that popped into his head. "Whales."

"Yes. Whales." Molly stared at the giant creatures as if in a daze, her voice drenched in awe. "Sea lions, puffins, Dall's porpoises, American black bear, snowshoe hares— and mountain goats too. They're all native species to this area."

"Thanks for another zoology lesson, Bolt."

She gave him a side-glance at his sarcastic tone and he grinned.

"Kidding. It's pretty here."

"It's beautiful."

Molly closed her eyes and inhaled deeply. All Jake could think of at that moment was her beneath him, arching, panting, crying out as she came undone in his arms.

"Almost makes me sad to leave."

Her words stirred something inside him. Deep down, his instincts told him he could find happiness with her and urged him to take a chance. Told him that despite their differences, and all the reasons why they shouldn't be together, things between them felt sort of…perfect.

"I'm sure Chicago's nice."

He gazed into the distance as Captain Fred moved them

into the larger fjords. A noisy flock of squawking seagulls filled the air and the crisp scent of sea water stung his nose. Hazy clouds had blown in with the stiff breeze off the glaciers, frosty and bleak.

Jake hunkered down in his jacket and shoved his hands into his pockets. "There's got to be more things to do in the big city than what we have here."

"Oh, it's fine. If you like those sorts of things."

"And you don't?"

"I like the museums and the theaters, and walking down by the lakeshore in the summer. But I'm not really much of a party girl."

"No?" he said, his tone dripping with mock horror.

"Yes." Her lilting giggle shivered through him like chimes. "I know it's hard to believe."

"What do you do on all those long Chicago nights, then?" He shouldn't have asked, but he couldn't seem to help himself. "Besides curing the incurable."

"I read. A lot. And I work."

"Sounds like a rollercoaster of thrills."

She chuckled. "You're one to talk."

The wind whipped her pale hair around her face beneath that impractical flouncy hat. No way Molly wasn't cold in that jacket, no matter how much it had cost her—which was too much, based on the fancy designer logo stitched on the front. Besides, Jake could think of much better ways to keep her warm—like with his arms, his body, his mouth and hands.

"From what I've heard, all you do is hang around the hospital and pick up extra shifts," Molly said. "You even admitted on the bus you're a shameless workaholic."

"Hmm…" Jake looked at her again. She was lovely. Lovely and infinitely touchable.

Her smile widened as weak sunlight filtered through the overcast skies. "Thanks for sharing about your past."

"Thanks for listening."

Jake jammed the toe of his hiking boot against the deck of the ship. Now wasn't the time to let his libido take charge. They were just getting familiar with each other, exploring this connection between them, figuring out if they wanted to take things further, deeper. He found himself trusting her more and more each day.

"And thanks for talking about your childhood with me."

"You're welcome."

"Your secrets are safe with me, Bolt."

"As are yours with me. My lips are sealed."

She made a little twisting motion with her fingers in front of her mouth, like turning a key then tossing it away, and his stubborn thoughts zoomed right back to other things she might do with those fingers, with that mouth…

"Ladies and gentlemen, in the distance you'll see a group of humpback whales bubble-netting," Captain Fred announced.

Jake moved in beside Molly again, his arm resting comfortably against hers.

"Bubble-netting is a cooperative effort by a pod of whales. They work together to encircle prey fish such as herring into a ball with bubbles. Then they swim up through it and trap the fish in their mouths, expelling the sea water as they breach the surface."

On cue, two of the humongous whales arched over the surface of the inlet and spouted enormous plumes of water high into the air. The mist drifted on the breeze to drizzle down on the passengers.

Molly gasped along with the rest of the tourists, then clapped with delight, snapping photos with her phone before pointing excitedly. "Did you see that?"

"I did."

But Jake was having as much fun watching Molly's reactions as he was the whales. In fact if there hadn't been so many people around he would've revisited that passionate kiss they'd shared in the gym, maybe taken things a bit farther—removed that ridiculous hat and plunged his hands into her hair, slipping his fingers beneath her coat and…

"How about I take a picture of the two of you together?" asked Joe, the captain's assistant.

"Uh…" Jake looked over at Molly, who nodded. "Okay. Sure."

"Great." Joe motioned for them to move closer. "Put your arm around her waist."

Jake did as he was instructed, pulling Molly into his side as she slipped her hand beneath his coat to hook her finger through the belt loops on his jeans. His whole nervous system jolted from her touch.

"Cool." Joe adjusted the camera angle. "All right. Let's see a smile from the happy couple."

"Oh, we're not a—" they both started in unison.

Snap. Snap. Snap.

"Awesome." Joe handed Molly her phone, then slapped Jake on the back. "You're a lucky man. Take care of her."

I will.

Jake watched Joe walk away, somewhat stunned at his inner response.

Molly stood across from him, frowning down at her phone screen.

"What? Are they awful?" he asked, moving in beside her again.

"No." She shoved the device back in her pocket before he could see what was on the screen. "I'm just… It's nice being here with you today. Spending time with you."

Funny how much her thoughts mirrored his own.

"My shooting schedule and difficult cases don't leave me much time outside of work. That's another reason why Brian left," Molly said, leaning against the railing again, staring out to sea. "His text said he doubted I'd even notice he was gone."

"And do you?"

"What?"

"Notice he's gone?"

"Honestly? I haven't—not really." She laughed, short and sweet, then smiled. "I've been too busy. Thanks to Bobby and a certain Head of Emergency Medicine."

Jake's body warmed with affection and he moved a tad closer to her to block the harsh wind, a now familiar surge of protectiveness joining the simmering passion inside him.

"When I was growing up, my mom always said love can't be rushed. That if you stop searching it'll happen."

"She sounds like a wise lady."

The earnestness in her voice made his heart clench. His scores in the lasting relationship department might not be stellar, but at least he'd been there, done that. The fact that Molly hadn't, made those staunch barriers Jake had built around himself crumble even more. Yes, she was leaving soon, and maybe whatever happened between them could only be temporary, but that didn't mean it couldn't also be real.

"I have a suggestion," Jake said, before common sense made him rethink his actions.

"What?"

"How about I take you to dinner when we get back to Anchorage? A true date this time."

"I was going to go to the hospital and check on Bobby."

Jake pulled out his phone and showed her a recent message. "Gladys says he's stable and resting comfortably."

Molly chewed on her bottom lip. "Are you sure?"

"More than anything, Bolt." He put his arm around her and cuddled her close, unable to resist any longer. Against all odds, God help him, his walls were crashing down. "More than anything."

CHAPTER NINE

"I JUST HAVE a bad headache," Molly said over the phone to Neal, doing her best to keep the guilt from her voice.

She still couldn't quite believe she'd agreed to go to dinner instead of going to the hospital. Yet here they were, back at Jake's favorite pub, splitting another order of salmon nachos. The tiny rebellion both thrilled and terrified her.

"I'm going to sleep it off and be ready to go again tomorrow."

"Hmm…" Neal said, his tone concerned. "Maybe it's a brain tumor."

"It's not a brain tumor." Five years of working on a medical reality TV show had made her crew into hypochondriacs.

She peered through the glass doors of the small lobby. Jake caught Molly's eye and waved. With a sigh, she tugged at her long-sleeved black T-shirt, this one proclaiming Bacteria—It's the only culture some people have, then smoothed her hand down her faded jeans.

"Listen, I need to get off the phone."

"Are you losing consciousness?" Neal said. "I'll dial 911."

"No. I'm fine. I'm going to take a hot bath and a couple of ibuprofen, then go to bed. I've instructed the hospital staff to call me if there are any changes to Bobby's condition. Talk to you later."

Before Neal could respond Molly shut off her phone, then walked back through the doors, joining Jake as the server placed a large platter of nachos and two sodas on the table.

Molly slid onto the bench seat across from him, shoving her pink coat into the corner to make more room. "Sorry."

"Everything okay?" he asked. "Nice shirt, by the way."

"Oh, thanks." Her snarky tees were one of her favorite means of creative expression. "Some people don't get my sense of humor."

"That's one of my favorite things about you, Bolt." He winked and her heart did a flip. "Hand me your plate."

"Thanks again for dinner."

"My pleasure." Jake handed Molly a heaping pile of nachos, his long legs nudging hers under the table. "Is that enough for you?"

"Pretty sure this is enough for four people." She tucked her hair behind her ear and stared down at her plate, suddenly shy. "I had an excellent time today."

"Me too." He passed her a fork, his fingers lingering longer than necessary. "Let's eat."

She'd been hungry before, but the spicy smell of the nachos made her famished. They both dug into the food with relish. Minutes went by, filled with small talk and lots of crunching as they devoured the Mexican treat.

At last Molly took a final bite then sat back, stuffed.

Jake grinned over at her. "You have something in the corner of your mouth."

"I do?" She wiped her lips. "Gone?"

"Nope." He pointed toward the right side of his face. "Right there."

Molly tried again. "Did I get it?"

"No." Jake shook his head, then reached for her napkin. "Here—let me."

She leaned forward, meeting him halfway across the table. Her gaze fell to his mouth as his fingertip grazed her skin.

"There…" he murmured, with unmistakable desire lighting his eyes.

"Thanks," she whispered, not pulling away.

"You're welcome." Jake closed the tiny gap between them and brushed his lips over hers.

The sound of a throat being cleared broke them apart.

"Sorry, folks," their server said. "I'll just leave the check here for whenever you're done."

Jake sat back, one dark brow cocked. "I'm ready. How about you?"

Molly nodded, her frenzied response to him raging higher.

"Great."

He flagged down the server and handed over cash before leading Molly from the pub. They'd left her Range Rover at the supercenter and driven here in Jake's truck. Once inside the vehicle, he started the engine and cranked the heater, turning out of the parking lot and heading in the opposite direction from her hotel.

"Where are we going?" Molly asked.

"I thought I'd show you my house."

Jake took her hand again, and the gentle stroke of his thumb against her skin sent a frisson of need through her body.

"Sound good?"

"Yes."

She stared out the window beside her as they zipped through the nighttime traffic, heading out of downtown Anchorage and into a residential neighborhood. He pulled into the driveway of a ranch-style home with lots of construction supplies stacked around the perimeter.

Jake cut the engine, then came around to help her out. "Excuse the mess. I'm doing some remodeling."

"No. It's great."

Molly's breath hitched as he kissed her against the side of the truck, the cold metal at her back at direct odds with the solid heat of Jake pressed to her front. She surrendered to the wonderful sensations storming through her—passion, affection, aching want.

At last he broke away, resting his forehead against hers. "I've wanted to do that again since that night in the gym."

"Me too." She smiled, tangling her fingers into the silky

curls at the nape of his neck, her pulse thudding and her knees weak.

Molly wanted him so much she hurt. This wasn't like her. This wasn't logical. This wasn't like anything she'd ever experienced before and she was loving every single second.

"C'mon." Jake led her to his front porch, then fumbled to get his key into the lock.

The notion that he might be as affected as she was made Molly giddy with hope. He tugged her inside and flipped on the lights, removing his coat and his flannel shirts to leave only the Henley behind.

"Let me show you around."

The open-concept interior of the house was exceptionally tidy for a bachelor pad, if a bit sparse. Tools and construction equipment filled several corners, but the kitchen was finished and well-appointed, with gleaming appliances and granite countertops. The floors were hardwood, shining as if newly waxed. The smell of sawdust and fresh paint tickled Molly's nose as she gazed around.

"You're doing all this yourself?"

"Yep. In my spare time."

"Right... All that spare time, huh?"

"Yeah." Jake gave Molly a self-deprecating grin, heading toward a large double-sided fridge. "Can I get you anything? Water? Wine?"

She shrugged out of her coat and hat, draping them over the back of a folding metal chair. What she really needed to find was a place to plug in her phone. "Got a place I can re-juice?"

"Sure."

Jake led her down the hall and into a master suite, complete with king-size bed and a large walk-in closet attached to a luxurious travertine-tiled bath.

"Right there." He pointed to a spot on the nightstand.

"Great." Molly plugged in her device, then straightened. The air crackled with sexual tension and her muscles were tight with need. She wanted to touch Jake, taste him, burrow beneath his rigid self-control and make him pant with desire. She'd never had this kind of amazing chemistry with anyone before and she longed to explore every facet.

As if reading her thoughts, Jake closed the slight distance between them, taking her hand. "I like you, Molly. A lot."

She rested her forehead on his chest, inhaling his comforting scent, and waited for the inevitable caveat that always followed such statements, whether from her father or Brian or any other man.

"Except you need me to work harder, or stop arguing, or—"

"No." Jake silenced her, placing his finger beneath her chin and forcing Molly to meet his gaze. "I like you. Just as you are."

Then he kissed her again, his strong arms pulling her close. His lips were demanding, yet gentle, and every cell in her body felt heavy and buoyant at the same time. Her head fell back as his mouth traveled down her neck to her pulse point and... Oh, my...

With Brian, sex had always felt a bit detached and, well... clinical. Now, though, Molly didn't know where to touch Jake first.

He took one of her fluttering hands, kissed her palm before placing it over his thudding heart, allowing her to feel just how much she affected him. His mouth returned to hers, deepening the kiss, tasting her, seducing her. His caresses grew hotter, more insistent, until he pulled away to stroke the hair back from her forehead.

She swayed closer and Jake cupped her cheek. "Do you want to go to bed with me?"

"Yes, please," Molly whispered, every nerve ending in her body poised on a precipice. "Are you sure you want to go to bed with me?"

"Oh, yeah, Bolt. I'm sure."

Jake smiled as he picked her up. Her legs wrapped around

his waist and her arms went around his neck and she returned his kisses, hard and deep. His low moans only served to stoke her passion higher. She couldn't get enough. She had to have more of him…would die without him.

Desperate, Molly pulled at his clothes, needing to get closer to this beautiful man who made her feel beautiful too.

Tearing his mouth from hers, Jake kissed his way down the side of her neck as he laid Molly on the bed, then stretched out beside her. His hands seemed to be everywhere at once—touching, stroking, undoing and removing things. Her T-shirt was the first to go, followed in short order by his Henley, and then she reveled in the first brush of his naked chest against her skin.

Jake made quick work of her bra too, cupping her bare breasts gently, his thumbs circling their sensitive pink tips while Molly, emboldened, slipped her hand between their bodies to feel his rigid length pressed tight against the front of his jeans.

He groaned softly while she caressed him through the soft material. His breathing grew raspier and she kissed him again. At last, he rolled her beneath him and she looped her legs around his waist once more, craving the feel of his hard body against her.

"This first time should be special, but I want you too badly. It's been too long."

"I want you too." Molly flicked open the top of his fly, then snuck her fingers inside his waistband. The zipper crept down slowly, to accommodate her touch as she traced the outline of his erection through his briefs. "So much."

His breath caught and his gaze was searing, hot and demanding. "Keep that up and I won't last."

"Endurance is overrated," she said, grinning.

Quickly discarding the rest of his clothes, Jake lowered himself beside her once more, reaching between her thighs to stroke her wet folds. Gently, he thrust first one, then two fingers inside her, while his thumb circled her most sensitive flesh, preparing her.

She whimpered, arching hard against his hand. He seemed to know exactly how to touch her, how to tease her to the brink of ecstasy in no time flat. Her orgasm loomed closer, closer, and she buried her face against his shoulder as her first climax struck.

"I've got you." He held her until her body quieted against him, then smoothed her hair from her flushed cheeks. "Good?"

"Amazing."

Molly pressed Jake down onto his back, straddling him. She wasn't a vixen, by any stretch, but she had to see him, touch him, taste him. In control, she grasped the hard, hot length of him, draping her hair over his chest and hips as she leaned forward and licked his skin, savoring the salty flavor.

"My turn…"

Molly's warm breath and tongue against his aching flesh was almost Jake's undoing. Then she engulfed him in the wet embrace of her mouth and he damned near passed out. He slipped his fingers through her silken hair while she pleasured him with her lips and tongue, but soon his need grew too strong to deny.

Unable to wait any longer, Jake rolled over, pinning Molly beneath him as he kissed a slow descent down her body, stopping along the way to pay homage to her delightful breasts, then nuzzling her navel before traveling lower.

She was everything he'd ever wanted and more. All creamy soft skin and dreamy soft sighs.

Gently he licked once, twice, over her heated core, making love to her with his mouth, only stopping when she'd reached her second climax. Then, at last, he kissed his way up her body until he settled atop her again.

Molly laced her fingertips in the hair at his nape, her bright blue eyes glittering with passion. An involuntary shudder ran through Jake at the soft caress. She reached for his hard length again, but he placed a restraining hand atop hers.

"Stop, or I won't last more than a few seconds." He nipped her earlobe. "And I want this to last forever."

Levering himself up on his elbows, Jake grabbed a condom from the nightstand drawer and smoothed it on before entering her in one long thrust. Molly moaned, the sound low and laced with satisfaction. Buried hilt-deep, he stilled, savoring the exquisite sensations.

"You feel amazing, sweetheart. You are amazing."

"S-so are you," she whispered, her gaze locked with his as he began a slow, steady rhythm, driving them both closer to the brink.

He loved the sexy catch in her voice. The way their lovemaking seemed to chase all coherent thought from her brilliant mind.

Molly ground against him, increasing the delicious friction. "Please…don't stop."

"Never."

He moaned as she clutched him closer, riding out the waves of another orgasm. Unable to deny himself any longer, Jake slipped his fingers through hers, his senses overwhelmed by her passion, her…everything.

Soon a familiar tightness filled his groin, signaling his looming release. Jake drove into Molly one last time before his body went whipcord-tight, a deep groan tearing from his lungs. He murmured her name again and again, lost in an endless avalanche of endorphins and pleasure.

As the intensity ebbed and drowsiness overtook him he rested his head in the valley between her breasts. He felt boneless, weightless, yet heavy as concrete, sated beyond belief as she toyed with his hair.

She always smelled like citrus and sunshine.

Like home.

He wanted to stay inside this heavenly private universe

and never come out. This was what he'd searched for and never found—this closeness, this connection, this trust. He struggled to keep his heavy-lidded eyes open, not wanting the moment to end.

Eventually Molly's breathing evened out into the pattern of sleep and Jake rolled to his side, spooning her against him beneath the covers before drifting into slumber.

CHAPTER TEN

MOLLY WOKE BEFORE dawn and looked over her shoulder at the man snoozing beside her. Jake Ryder was one sexy beast. No doubt about it. In fact she couldn't stop admiring the gorgeous corded muscles in his strong arms, the design of his tattoo visible on the tanned perfection of his left bicep. Couldn't stop admiring the chiseled lines of his back as he hugged the pillow beneath him, admiring the way his torso formed a perfect V down to his slim waist, then dipped into his lower back.

She eyed the covers. If he moved slightly those sheets might reveal the tight globes of his butt too.

Molly grinned like a dope as she stared up at the ceiling. What a spectacular night.

She was no blushing virgin—she and Brian had lived together, after all—but the difference between him and Jake was like sun and shadow. Brian had never been one to take the lead—or to take his time. Jake had no problem being an alpha male—in the sack or out. And yet he'd taken all the time in the world to make Molly feel exquisite. The things they'd done to each other had been hot and sexy and…well…sweet.

Memories of him came: his dark curls sweaty and his cheeks flushed, his muscles shaking from tension and release as he collapsed beside her and murmured endearments into her hair. Her insides fluttered just from thinking about it.

Then her phone buzzed from the nightstand and her bubble of sublime happiness burst.

Yesterday, out in the wilderness, it had been easy to forget about reality. But now the world seemed determined to crash in at every turn, chipping away at the tiny utopia they'd created.

Molly rubbed her eyes and groaned. Coffee. She needed liquid energy before she could face the world again.

Carefully she slipped out from between the sheets and used the bathroom before tugging on her clothes and then fumbling her way down the unfamiliar hall. There were only a few hints of the coming dawn in the sky, so it must still be super-early. She stumbled into his kitchen and clicked on the lights, squinting into the brightness as she searched for the necessary supplies to make a pot.

Once finished, Molly tiptoed back into the bedroom to grab her phone and charger, then returned to the kitchen, where she scrolled through what appeared to be a gazillion messages from her crew, asking her to call in immediately. Man, a girl takes one day off and everything goes nuts.

After a resigned sigh, Molly dialed Rob's number. "Hey, it's me."

"Have you seen the announcement?" her cameraman asked, his voice a tad panicked.

"What announcement?"

"Promise me you won't look until you get here."

"Seriously?" Molly sighed heavily, leaning her hip against the island and tapping her stockinged toes against the chilly hardwood floor. "Is Neal there?"

"He can't come to the phone."

"Why not?"

"He's on a conference call with Les Montgomery and—"

"The head of the MedStar Network?" Molly straightened, her pulse kicking a notch higher. "About what?"

"Hang on." Murmured voices echoed through the line before Rob returned. "Just get to the hospital as fast as you can—okay?"

He hung up before she could respond.

Crap.

Molly walked into the living room to tug on her boots

and clicked on the lights there too. Rob tended to be a bit of a drama queen when it came to network gossip, so she wasn't going to freak out quite yet about his urgent request for her to get to Anchorage Mercy stat, but she did want to return soon anyway, to check on Bobby.

After tugging on her footwear, she spotted a group of photos on one wall, near the windows. The first showed a young Jake—maybe four or five—with a man and woman she guessed were his parents. The man had the same dark hair and gray eyes and the woman shared her son's devilish grin.

Next was the same group shot, but all of them were older, in front of a large RV. This time Jake held a gorgeous brunette in his arms. From the besotted expression on his face and the way his lips were pressed to the girl's cheek, Molly guessed this had to be the infamous Kellie.

The third picture showed Jake again, handsome and serious in his dress uniform. And was that the President, pinning a gold medal on his chest? He'd briefly mentioned receiving an award for his service in the Army but nothing like this.

Molly moved on to the last photo. This one had to be his beloved regiment—a group of about twenty men and women. Jake and Bobby were near the middle of the back row, easily the tallest guys in the group. Jake's eyes sparkled with mischief and one side of his mouth was curved in that sweet smile she was quickly coming to know.

To know and love…

Pulse thudding, Molly raised a shaky hand to her face. She liked Jake—much more than was probably wise. They were compatible in many ways, but had she fallen for him?

The sound of footsteps echoed behind her and she turned to find Jake leaning against the doorframe. His broad chest was distractingly bare above a pair of worn sweatpants that hinted at far more than they concealed.

"What's going on?" he asked, his voice sleepy and deliciously rough.

Her phone buzzed again and Molly squinted down at a text from Neal.

Get in here. Now.

Right. Work. She thumbed in a quick response.

On my way.

"Is it Bobby?" Jake moved closer, rubbing his eyes before glancing down at her screen.

"No. My crew. Something's going on with the network." Molly shut the device off, doing her best not to stare at Jake's amazing torso on full display. At the muscles she'd love to stroke and kiss and nuzzle all over again.

Get your head back in the game, Flynn.

She exhaled and looked away. "I need to get back to the hospital."

"That's too bad," Jake said. "I was hoping we could spend time together this morning."

Me too...

A "ding" issued from the coffeemaker and the rich smell of fresh-brewed coffee filled the air. They walked into the kitchen and Jake poured them each a large mug. Toes curled and eyes lowered, Molly sipped her brew and struggled to express how much last night had meant.

With Brian, she'd always gone to work early, maybe leaving a small note on the nightstand, asking him to pick something up for dinner. Quick exits made for fewer awkward conversations about things neither of them wanted to discuss.

But with Jake Molly wanted to talk about all sorts of things—birthdays, favorite colors, favorite foods, if he rooted for the Cubs or the White Sox. Go Cubbies. With Jake she cared—much more than she was ready to admit. Of course it didn't help when he stood there, rumpled and perfect and nice and naughty all rolled into one.

Jake watched her over the rim of his coffee cup, his gaze far too perceptive.

Beneath his scrutiny Molly's analytical mind kicked in again, blaring with all too familiar warning bells.

Slow down, step back, assess and strategize.

While her heart demanded the opposite.

Cuddle. Snuggle. Ravish. Repeat.

Flustered, Molly set her half-finished coffee on the counter and inched toward the hallway. "I…um…should get going."

Not the most eloquent parting words, but considering the war going on inside her she'd been lucky to say anything coherent.

"Right." Jake put his mug aside as well, following her. "About last night…"

Uh-oh. That statement was never good.

Molly held her breath, not sure she'd survive if Jake said what she feared he might say—that what they'd shared had been a mistake instead of the best, most emotionally moving experience of her life.

The realization of her true feelings for Jake sent shockwaves through Molly's system. She'd promised to stay safe, stay unattached, stay un-entangled, and here she was in—

Nope. Not saying that word.

Nope. Nope. Nope.

But her rebel thoughts refused to cooperate, flooding her mind with fresh images of them in his bed, touching, tasting, lost in each other in the darkest hours before dawn.

Adrenaline mixed with the ache in her chest and Molly stumbled backward, darting a glance at Jake and then instantly regretting her decision. His firm lips were quirked into that sexy little half-grin as he crowded into her personal space with one dark brow arched.

"No need to panic, Bolt. I only bite when asked."

Stunned into silence, Molly watched as he placed one hand on either side of her on the doorframe, his chest brushing against her with blatant seduction. She bit her lip and stared at his tanned throat. If she rose on tiptoes she could nuzzle that spot below his ear…the one she'd discovered made him shiver.

Her phone was buzzing, buzzing, buzzing and her mind was distracted. Her anxiety skyrocketed. She blinked hard, unwanted facts clogging her mind before they tumbled out in a torrent of embarrassment.

Cue awkward rambling in three…two…one…

"Contrary to popular belief, penguins do not live at the North Pole, or anywhere in the northern hemisphere, including Alaska. Also, Magellanic penguins are monogamous and have the same mates for life."

Jake's gaze flew to hers and Molly's heart raced like a hamster on a wheel.

Please don't make fun of me. Please don't make me feel like an outsider. Please.

"Um…wow. Okay." His eyes narrowed. "Are you telling me you enjoyed last night?"

"I…uh…" Feeling totally exposed, Molly rushed to the living room to gather her things before barreling for the front door. She paused halfway out on the porch. "I'll see you at the hospital."

She left before Jake could respond.

It would've been a movie-perfect departure too—except she'd forgotten he'd driven last night and her Rover was still back in the supercenter parking lot.

Fabulous.

Breath frosting in the early-morning air, Molly trudged back to the front door and found Jake waiting, arms crossed and smile patient. "Can you give me a ride to my car?"

"Be with you in five minutes, Bolt." His tone was laced with mirth.

The wait, at least, gave Molly time to gulp down the rest of her coffee and sort through her emails.

Jake joined her in his living room with ninety seconds to spare, having showered and pulled on fresh jeans and a black crewneck sweater. As he bent to shove his feet into his boots she couldn't help staring one last time at his marvelous physique. The man was gorgeous and wonderful, and the fact she'd spent the whole night with him still seemed a bit unreal.

"Ready?" Jake asked, slipping on his coat.

"Ready." Molly nodded, doing her best to regain her mental equilibrium.

She was back on duty. Time to think of Bobby and her career. Time to put her needs and wants second.

They walked out to his truck, which was covered in the thin layer of frost that had formed during the wee hours. Jake cranked the engine while Molly grabbed a scraper to brush off his windshield. Soon they were on their way, rumbling down the road as the heater struggled to warm them.

This early, it seemed wildlife was everywhere. She'd not paid much attention the night before, but Jake's property abutted the Chugach National Forest. Trees towered overhead and a large hawk swooped amongst the boughs, hunting for a meal. She even spotted a fox with kits darting through the foliage.

"This place is amazing," she said, pulling out her phone to snap a few shots.

"I love it." Jake smiled. "Alaska's home. Can't imagine living anywhere else."

Molly suppressed a pang of sadness. Yet another reason she should check her feelings at the door and just enjoy last night for what it had been. A one-time occurrence. A fling. She had a career in Chicago. Jake had deep roots here in

Anchorage. Long-distance relationships never worked. And hadn't Brian complained he never got to see her as it was?

She was still mulling this over as they pulled into the supercenter lot and Jake parked beside her Range Rover.

Molly unfastened her seat belt and grabbed the metal door handle, feeling its icy chill through her gloves as she hesitated, unsure what to say. "Um… I had a wonderful time."

Jake nodded, staring at the shopping center beyond. Only a few determined bargain-hunters were heading out this early in the morning.

"Maybe we can have lunch together later? To talk?"

His rough, deep voice made her knees go weak again.

Yes. "Maybe. Depends on my schedule. Text me and I'll let you know."

Molly started to climb out—only to be pulled back into the truck and against Jake's chest. His soft lips found hers and he kissed her deeply, leaving them both breathless. He smelled of soap and shampoo from his recent shower, and when he lifted his head, his pupils were dilated, nearly obscuring his stormy gray irises.

Molly bit her lip and Jake tracked the tiny movement, frown lines forming between his dark brows. She pressed her palms against his chest and forced herself to move away, before she ended up surrendering to temptation.

"See you later."

"Yeah," he said, his voice husky. "See you later, Bolt."

Jake waited until she'd gotten the Range Rover started, and was still waiting when Molly pulled out of the lot and headed toward her hotel. His image grew smaller and smaller in the rearview mirror as her uncertainty grew and grew. She should turn around. She should go back. She should call her crew and tell them she'd be there when she was ready.

Molly kept driving. Her career and her patient were waiting at the hospital. She needed to shower and change and then get back to work. Lives depended on her skills, her genius.

Last night had been a singular fantasy, a brilliant one-time dream.

The sooner Molly remembered that, the better.

Jake sat for a long while after Molly left, just thinking. He wasn't due back at the ER for several hours and his thoughts, along with his heart, seemed jumbled.

Last evening he'd allowed himself to let go with Molly, to feel more, both physically and emotionally. By trusting her, he'd allowed himself to be vulnerable. He'd never imagined he'd get to that point again after what had happened with Kellie, but he had—a hell of a lot faster than he'd expected too. The time he and Molly had spent together these past few weeks had allowed him to see past her hard candy shell and vice versa. He'd glimpsed the real woman beneath her professional persona—a woman with wants and needs, a past and a future. A woman who was smart and interesting and well-spoken.

And, yeah, a bit quirky too. Loveably quirky.

He chuckled at the memory of her penguin outburst. Funny thing was, Jake had taken an online test once, in a college freshman Psych course, to find out what animal best fit his personality. Turned out he was indeed a penguin—witty, meticulous, intelligent, inscrutable.

Yep. That about summed him up.

After starting the engine, Jake headed back toward his house again—only to step on his brakes as a family of Canadian geese waddled across the main roadway. While he waited for the feathered pedestrians to move past, Molly's remark about penguins mating for life swirled in his brain. Why had she chosen that fact to spout? Was she interested in forever with him?

He sighed and accelerated once the geese had passed—only to stop at a red light.

Nah. Molly couldn't want a future with him. She had her TV show, a busy career. The last thing she'd want was to live out here on the wild frontier.

Besides, last night was a one-time deal. He'd gone into this knowing full well what he was getting into. To wish for anything more would just be courting disaster, no matter how spectacular those hours with Molly in his arms had been. No matter how scorching the sex or how funny and smart and fascinating she was. That was no reason to go off the deep end and get his heart broken again when she left.

Right?

Jake passed a slower moving car before signaling back into his lane, feeling that ache of indecision returning. Dammit. He'd hoped to sit down with Molly and talk this morning before heading into work, maybe figure out how to handle this thing between them—have a chance to make sure that they were on the same page, that he wasn't missing something important like it felt he was.

As he turned down the road leading to his house once again Jake decided to let it rest. He'd text her for lunch later, just as he'd said. Then they'd meet in the cafeteria and discuss things rationally, objectively. Hearts and emotions uninvolved.

CHAPTER ELEVEN

By the time Molly reached the hospital the churning unease in her gut was threatening to boil over. The fact that there were multiple emergency vehicles blocking the front entrance didn't help either.

She pulled over to the curb and got the attention of one of the police officers to let her through. "What's going on?"

"Grizzly cub slipped through the automatic doors. Momma followed her baby inside, causing a ruckus," the officer said, tipping his hat when she flashed her physician's badge. "No worries, Doc. No one was hurt, and the conservation officers have the bears tranquilized and caged. We'll be airlifting them to a safer location away from the city soon."

Molly shook her head. "Never had that happen back in Chicago."

"I should hope not." The cop grinned and waved her through toward the physicians' parking area. "Have a good day, Doc."

"Thanks."

Molly pulled around the building and into a spot, then hurried to the fourth floor. The elevator doors opened to reveal Neal and Rob, looking nervous.

"All right—what's going on?" she asked as they all headed for her office. "If the network's canceling my show, please tell me. I can handle it. This was the last episode on my current contract anyway."

"No, Mol." Neal closed the door behind them. "They're not cancelling your show. You want the bad news or the worse news first?"

"Bad."

"Okay. They're giving your father a show of his own."

"What?" The world seemed to tilt on its axis and Molly slumped into her chair, coat half-off. All those years of work to escape him, and now he was taking over her territory. "His own show? On my network?"

"Yep." Rob looked pained. "And there's more."

"More?" Shock had made Molly into a parrot.

"They're giving him the prime spot right after Diagnosis Critical."

"I'll be my father's lead-in?"

"Don't think of it like that, Mol." Neal winced. "You're already established and you have a loyal, if small, audience base. Nothing's going to change."

Nothing would change?

Everything would change if Roger Flynn joined the Med-Star Network.

Molly swallowed against the rising bile in her throat. Losing her show because it had failed on its own merits was one thing. Having it forced into cancellation by her own father would be beyond awful. Forget fumbling and flailing in front of his small group of assembled guests at their house when she'd been a kid. This time her epic fail would happen on a global scale.

Molly hung up her coat, then took her seat again, the news still refusing to sink in. Gone. The sweet refuge of her show, the years she'd spent building it, growing it, sacrificing her time and effort and any semblance of a normal life. All gone.

"Trust me, Mol. This isn't the end of the world." Neal placed a hand on her shoulder. "I bet this hoopla will blow over and things will get back to normal soon."

"This is not going to blow over."

Molly knew her father. For him, things were all or nothing. Roger Flynn wouldn't be satisfied until he was number one on the network, no matter who he had to crush along the way—including his own daughter.

"I need to think about things for a moment. Alone."

The two men exchanged a look and her heart sank even further.

Eyes closed, Molly braced herself. "Fine. Tell me the rest of it."

Rob cringed. "Well…about that footage."

"What footage?"

"The footage of Dr. Ryder we've shot over the weeks—the stuff the network was supposed to edit out. It got leaked."

"Leaked?" Molly frowned. "To who?"

"The world." Rob glanced over at Neal. "Snippets turned up on the Internet."

The enormity of the situation engulfed her, seizing the air in Molly's lungs. "Jake could sue us. He never signed the releases."

He trusted me.

Molly clutched the edge of her desk to keep herself from crumpling. "Who leaked it?"

"The network blames one of the interns," Neal said. "And their attorneys are going to use implied consent as their defense, since Dr. Ryder knew we were filming and stayed anyway."

"That's flimsy, at best," Molly said, her voice quiet.

Jake had trusted her. That was huge, after everything that had happened with his commendation and with Kellie. Sorrow squeezed her chest tight. The future of their relationship was now solidified. Once he discovered the truth he'd never want to see her again. And rightfully so.

But she wasn't ready to let him go yet, not when she'd just found him.

Neal pulled off his baseball hat and scrubbed a hand through his graying hair. "If it's any consolation, the clips are popular. Hit the number one search spots on the big search engines and social media sites."

"No." Molly covered her face with her hands. "It's really not."

"We're sorry, Mol," Rob said, head lowered. "If there's anything we can do…"

"I know," she mumbled, and her crew left the office at last.

This was going to require some major damage control and Molly honestly had no idea where to start.

She needed to pull her contract with the network and make serious decisions about her show. She needed to check in on Bobby and make sure he was doing all right this morning. She needed to talk to Jake and beg his forgiveness, even though none of this was really her fault. But she was sure Jake wouldn't see it that way. It was her name, her face on the show. It had been her in his bed—her he'd trusted. Therefore, this debacle was her responsibility.

In the end, overwhelmed and frozen with fear, Molly sat and stared at the blank wall, wondering how a day that had started off so beautifully could crash and burn so fast.

After eating a quick breakfast and checking his emails, Jake headed to Anchorage Mercy. The traffic light turned green and he made a right toward the hospital—then halted as a line of departing squad cars blocked the main entrance.

A conservation truck pulled up next to him and the driver waved. "Had some bears in the lobby again, Doc. Got 'em out, though, no problem."

Jake nodded, appreciating the update, and waited until the rest of the traffic had cleared. At last he looped around to the back of the hospital and pulled into the spot beside Molly's Range Rover. He felt a sudden, yearning ache around his heart and…damn. Maybe sleeping with her hadn't been such a brilliant idea after all—not if he felt this attached to her, this fast.

After cutting the engine, Jake climbed from his truck and braced himself against the brisk wind. Their torrid night had stirred up all kinds of emotions—happiness, confusion, joy, fear. All those feelings had mixed together now, into a scary sludge inside him that made him wary as hell. He kept reminding himself that this wasn't the past and Molly wasn't Kellie. This was a new situation, with new rules, a new outcome.

The tension inside him didn't abate.

Maybe it was this whole thing with Bobby. He just wanted his best bud healthy again.

Jake swiped his physician's badge at the door, then headed inside. Technically, his shift wasn't scheduled to start for another hour, but he was sure another stack of paperwork awaited. Besides, he figured being at work would keep him from dwelling on what had happened with Molly last night—how she'd felt wrapped tight in his arms, how she'd made those delicious tiny gasps as he'd licked and kissed every single inch of her...

Wendy ran toward him down the hall. "Dr. Flynn's been trying to contact you. Bobby's heart-rate is irregular again."

Frowning, Jake pulled out his cell phone. The battery was dead. Normally he plugged it in each night like clockwork, but he hadn't followed his normal routine the previous evening.

Damn.

Jake sprinted upstairs and rushed into Bobby's room. Molly was checking his vitals while her crew filmed from the corner. Neither Neal nor Rob would meet his gaze. Jake thought that was weird, since he'd thought they'd become friendlier over the past few weeks, but he couldn't worry about them now. Not when Bobby's life was at stake.

"What's happening?"

"No idea. The tachycardia came up without warning," Molly said. The heart monitor beeped loud then went flat. She checked Bobby's pupils. "Start CPR and get a defibrillator stat!"

While Molly pumped air into Bobby's lungs, using an oxygen mask and bag, Jake started chest compressions. His best friend couldn't die. Not here. Not now. Not like this. Not after what they'd survived together back in the desert.

"Hang in there, buddy. Stay with me."

"Cart's here," Gladys said, shoving the machine up to the bedside.

"Get ready to shock him," Molly said. A sharp whine sounded as the paddles charged. "Stand back."

She jolted Bobby's heart with the electric current and his large body jerked. The monitor blipped. Stopped. Blip-blipped again. Grew stronger and more regular. Jake exhaled loudly as Molly set the paddles aside.

"Okay. We have a pulse. Gladys, start him on oxygen and watch him closely."

Jake took a deep breath to calm his own racing pulse, then followed Molly out into the hall. "I don't understand. Bobby was fine earlier."

"Could be residual effects from the yohimbe." Molly washed her hands in a nearby sink, not meeting his gaze. "But I won't know until his latest bloodwork comes back."

His earlier surge of adrenaline evaporated, leaving a trail of confusion and restlessness in its wake. Jake wanted to decompress, deconstruct, dissect all that had happened with Molly, but she was acting distant and distracted. Yep. Something was definitely up.

His wariness grew. And as her crew trundled out of Bobby's room, Jake pulled her aside. "Listen, Molly. I—"

"I'm sorry, but I—I can't do this right now."

Her voice had turned brittle, broken. Because of him? Because of what they'd shared last night?

The ache of tension inside Jake intensified, his doubts deepening. Maybe this whole thing about penguins and monogamy and a possible future with her was just a pipe dream. Maybe he'd been wrong too trust her so quickly.

That's your past talking.

"I'll keep you posted on the patient's condition." Molly

headed for the elevators and gestured toward her crew to follow. "C'mon, guys."

Jake headed back to his ER alone, feeling decidedly unsettled. After what had happened with Bobby, and with Molly pulling away the same way Kellie had just before the end, he was left feeling even more on edge.

CHAPTER TWELVE

THE NEXT DAY one thing was abundantly clear.

Molly couldn't tell Jake about the leaked footage—at least not as she'd originally planned. Never mind that the network's attorneys had expressly forbidden her to say anything. Truth was, she didn't know how to explain what had happened—didn't have the first clue how to apologize for a betrayal that would most likely destroy any bond they might have formed that night in his bed.

Not to mention that since making love with Jake Molly had discovered all sorts of uncomfortable, unruly, unexplored emotions jostling and poking inside her like sharp needles. Part of her couldn't suppress the flush of happiness each time she remembered their incredible lovemaking. But another part felt a deep twinge of guilt over the same.

Perhaps if Molly had stayed here at the hospital—not gone on the whale-watching cruise, not spent the night with Jake, Bobby wouldn't have taken a turn for the worse.

Until recently work had always come first. Now, though, for at least that one day and night, she'd decided to put her own wants and needs first and perhaps that hadn't been wise. Her father's censorious voice kept ringing through Molly's head, deriding her for allowing her emotions to gain the upper hand, ridiculing her because she'd failed to remain cool, aloof, unfeeling.

But those few hours in Jake's arms were the first time Molly had felt truly alive in…forever.

And once she told him about the leaked footage it would all be over.

Molly wasn't sure she could survive squeezing herself back into the tiny box her family had put her in for her whole life—not when she'd finally experienced such blissful freedom with Jake.

My Jake.

Her heart ached and her head hurt and the whole mess left her sad and off-balance.

She finished going over Bobby's chart notes and lab results again while Gladys checked the patient's IV. Rob and Neal stood in the corner, catching all the details for digital posterity. At least Bobby had bounced back again, now awake and alert despite the previous night's episode.

"Man." Bobby scooted up in his bed amidst a sea of tubes and monitor wires. "Can't believe that tea caused all my problems. I thought it was just some health supplement."

"Supplements are chemicals too, Mr. Templeton." Molly jotted down a few reminders for the staff, then closed his file. "And the tea didn't cause all your problems. It only added an additional symptom that masked the underlying disease process."

"Come again? I thought you said the heart thing was unrelated?"

"It is."

"I'm confused."

Rob moved closer to get a dramatic close-up of Bobby and Molly.

"The cardiac arrest you experienced the first time in the ER and again last evening was directly related to the yohimbe in the tea. Now that we've taken it out of the equation, and the chemical is leaving your body, we can concentrate on the real cause of your problems. Allergies."

"Allergies?" Bobby wrinkled his nose. "You mean like hay fever?"

"There are many types of allergies, Mr. Templeton. It will take time to narrow down the specific irritant responsible for yours. But because this allergy has gone untreated for so long, it's likely moved beyond simple watery eyes to a full-blown systemic issue. Your body's natural defenses have been compromised, diminishing your ability to heal. Those same defenses may have also caused damage to your organs."

"But I was tested for allergies a long time ago, Doc." Bobby gripped the sheets tighter. "Nothing came back positive. I don't want to be a human pin cushion. Needles aren't my favorite."

Molly raised a brow. For a man who regularly participated in mayhem on the ice, it seemed silly for him to fear a few epidermal scratches. Then again, most phobias weren't logical.

Take her fear of her father. In her mind, Molly knew she shouldn't let the man bully her anymore. She was a grown adult, more than capable of defending herself. But deep in her heart Molly still felt like that same scared little girl who had longed for her father's approval and love. Which was a wasted effort because he'd proved time and again that the only thing Roger Flynn loved was himself. His takeover of her network was only the latest in a long line of selfish acts.

"The good news is you'll have a few days to decide, Mr. Templeton." Molly scowled down at the orders clipped to the front of Bobby's chart, shoving all disturbing thoughts about her father aside. "It's too soon to test you at this point. The results would show false positives due to your high reactivity."

"I'm radioactive?" Bobby looked stunned.

"Not radioactive. Reactive. It means the antigen levels in your blood are too high to give us accurate results at this point. So we'll stabilize you, isolate you from all possible allergens, and give your body time to recuperate before proceeding."

"Uh…okay. How will that work?"

"We'll put you in a clean room," Molly said, glancing up at him.

Bobby surveyed the space. "This one looks pretty spotless to me."

"No. A clean room is sterile. Even the air is filtered to prevent any outside contamination. It's the only way for us to find out what's really causing your illness." She smiled and laid a hand on his arm to reassure him. "Visitation will be limited to a glassed-in area, where people can talk with you through special vents, unless they're wearing full protective gear."

"It'll be like a prison, then?"

"Think of it more as a spa. With lots of time to reflect. Maybe catch up on your sleep."

Bobby exhaled loudly. "All right—if it's the only way I can get better. The new season starts in a few weeks and I need to get in fighting shape by then or we've got no chance at the championship."

"Oh." She looked over to see her crew shaking their heads in despair. "Right…"

"Dr. Flynn?" Gladys peeked her head around the door. "Dr. Ryder's here to see you."

Her heart did a little somersault. "Thank you. I'll be right out. Do you have any other questions for me, Mr. Templeton?"

"No. Thanks."

"And, cut!" Neal said.

Rob lowered his camera and the two men followed her out of the room. Molly veered toward the nurses' station, then stopped abruptly at the sight of Jake bent over the counter. Heat unfurled within her again before she tamped it down.

Molly took a deep breath and handed the file to the nurse. "The orders for Mr. Templeton are inside."

Jake peered back at her over his shoulder. "Hey."

"Hey." She resisted the urge to fidget under his stare. "What are you doing?"

"I'm on a break and decided to check on Bobby."

He looked far more tempting than a man should be allowed to in faded green cotton as he read the file over Gladys's shoulder.

"A clean room?"

"It's the only way to confirm what's causing Bobby's allergic reactions."

"Agreed."

"Wonders never cease." Molly headed for her office.

"I know, right?" Jake chuckled, walking beside her. "Tell me when they're ready to move Bobby and I'll help get him situated."

"Are you expecting problems?"

"No. But he'll put up a fight when you try to take away his essentials."

"Essentials?"

"TV. Sports Illustrated."

"Hmm…" Molly stopped at her office door, facing him. "I never really considered it before, but it will be hard, being so isolated and alone."

"Uh-oh." Jake narrowed his gaze.

"What?"

"Be careful, Bolt. I think your empathy's showing."

"I have empathy. A great deal, in fact."

His words hurt more than she cared to admit. She'd been working on improving her bedside manner and had thought she was getting better. Jake could've helped her with that. He was so good with his patients, so caring and concerned.

Too bad he'd hate her once he found out about those leaked clips.

Shoulders slumped, Molly tucked her hair behind her ear. "I've already explained to the patient that it's only for a short while."

"Is everything okay?" Jake asked, his expression concerned. "Not just with Bobby."

"Of course." She forced a smile, swallowing the words that needed to be said. "Why?"

"You seem troubled." Jake took her hand, his thumb

stroking her knuckles and driving her to distraction. "We never really discussed what happened between us the other night. Want to have dinner with me later and we can talk?"

Her heart pinched at his earnest tone. She wanted to...oh, did she want to. But she'd already agreed to another conference call with the network attorneys, and if she had dinner with Jake she'd be tempted to tell him about the network's mistake, and then all this would be over and she'd be banished back to her cold, emotionless box.

Jake must have mistaken her silence for refusal, because he let her go, his smile fading and a glint of hurt flashing in his eyes. "If you don't want to go, just say so, Bolt. No big deal."

"No, no. It's not that." Her nervous babbling started. "I just need to see how things go today with my meetings, and I'm sure your schedule is nuts too, and I don't want Bobby to be alone because this could be a very scary time for him, and—"

The sudden heat returning to Jake's eyes took Molly's breath away. He leaned closer, as if he was going to kiss her. "Aw...there it is again."

"What?" Her voice emerged as a soft sigh of need, her lips tingling, waiting.

"Empathy. Compassion."

"I'm trying." Molly blinked, wishing she could just burrow into his arms until all this blew over and it was just the two of them, together.

"I know." Jake brushed the backs of his fingers over her cheek, his expression wistful. "Wonders never cease."

"What do they mean, I can't watch ESPN?" Bobby said, his voice horrified.

"No contamination. That means no TV, no books, no magazines, no nothing." Jake leaned back in the plastic chair beside his friend's bed and scrubbed a hand over his face.

"How about my phone?" Bobby's tone grew desperate. "The screen's kind of tiny, but I could still watch the recaps."

"Which part of 'no contamination' didn't you understand? Sorry, man."

"What am I supposed to do in there while I'm being clean?" Given the slight edge that had crept into Bobby's question, his normally affable friend had clearly taken a turn for the cranky. "She mentioned reflecting, or something, but that's not really my thing."

"How about resting? Enjoying the peace and quiet?"

"That's all I've been doing. Doesn't seem to be working out too good so far."

"Molly will find your diagnosis, bud. I'm sure of it. She's pretty brilliant."

"Molly, huh?" His best friend gave him some serious side-eye. "Since when are you and my new doctor on a first-name basis?"

Jake glanced out the open door and into the hallway beyond. He hadn't meant to let that informality slip, but it was too late to take it back. "We've developed a professional relationship, that's all."

"Professional?" Bobby snorted. "From the sappy look on your face, I'd say it's way more than that. Good for you. About time you got back in there after Kellie."

Jake bristled slightly at the mention of his ex. "Look, I'm just doing my job, and getting along with Dr. Flynn is part of it."

The response was lame, but he wasn't ready to share the things he felt for Molly. They were still too new, too fragile, too tender.

"You should thank me."

"Yeah, right. Thanks for getting me locked in my own private version of hell."

"It won't be any worse than the day we spent in the major general's office after we pranked the sergeant. Remember?"

Bobby's scowl was slowly transformed into a grin.

"Yeah... Still don't regret turning that guy into a Smurf. He was a real piece of work."

"Agreed." Jake pushed to his feet and headed for the door. His break time was almost over and he needed to get back to the ER. "I'll check on you later—once they get you moved."

"Okay." Bobby waited until Jake was almost out the door before calling. "Hey?"

"Yeah?"

"Thanks. For everything."

Jake's throat tightened. He owed Bobby more than he could ever repay. "I'm the one who should be thanking you, bud. You know that. Try and relax. This will all be over soon, I promise." Jake pointed to the TV against the wall. "And take advantage of the sports channels while you can."

A busy afternoon loomed ahead, with miles of paperwork to go before he was done. As Jake headed downstairs he still hoped Molly would take him up on his offer of dinner. Her earlier aloofness bothered him, and he missed her more than he cared to admit.

The emotional connection they'd shared since their night together had been stronger than anything he'd ever experienced with anyone—honestly. And, yes, distancing themselves might be the wise move, but, dammit, he wanted to talk to Molly, see her again, spend time with her even if it was only temporary.

Frustrated, Jake pulled out his phone in the elevator and sent her a text.

Dinner tonight? Eight p.m.

Surprisingly, Molly responded before he'd reached his office.

Okay.

Not sure what had changed her mind, but feeling extremely grateful something had, he messaged back, unable to keep the smile off his face.

Pick you up at your hotel.

Grinning wide, Jake shoved his phone into the pocket of his scrub shirt. He knew he was acting like a randy teenager, but it had been so long since he'd let someone close, as he had Molly, and it felt good. It seemed Wendy had been right. Putting himself out there again had given him a new lease on life.

Speaking of his favorite nurse—she stopped him as he passed her desk.

"There's someone waiting in your office." Instead of her usual sunny smile Wendy's expression held hints of anger and apology.

"Who?" he asked. "From your scowl, I'm guessing the answer's not good."

"Hello, Jake," said a female voice—one he'd never expected to hear again.

Stomach nosediving, he found Kellie standing in his office doorway. The woman who'd trampled his heart and his trust—who'd left him behind so fast he still had the tire marks down his back.

"What are you doing here?"

"Work." Kellie's smile was bland. "Can we talk? In private."

Wendy gave Jake a warning look, but he nodded, still in shock. "Uh…sure."

They walked into his office and he closed the door. Kellie settled into one of the chairs in front of his desk, her deep fuchsia power suit neon-bright under the fluorescent lights, her unreadable face made up to perfection.

Jake took his own seat, feeling like quarry avoiding a

hunter's crosshairs. "Big news story here in Anchorage, Alaska?"

"Up in Fairbanks, actually. I'm covering the transplant surgery being done at one of the hospitals there by Dr. Roger Flynn."

His phone buzzed and Jake pulled it out to see another text from Molly.

We need to talk.

The tension in his gut knotted tighter. Talking didn't have to mean anything bad. Just because those were the same words the woman across the desk from him had used the day she'd changed the trajectory of Jake's life forever, it didn't mean dinner with Molly would be more of the same.

He set his phone aside. Kellie was his past. Molly, hopefully, might be his future. And, yes, they had issues to work out—like how to deal with the whole long-distance thing— but they'd figure it out together. Life was all about communication.

He coughed to clear his throat. "I don't see what your story has to do with me."

Kellie's smile widened into an insincere affair that only made him yearn for Molly even more. "You're working a case with his daughter currently, aren't you? After seeing the footage of the two of you all over the Internet, I thought perhaps you could provide—"

"I'm sorry." Jake scowled, time seeming to warp around him. "What are you talking about? What footage?"

Surely those old stories about his commendation hadn't resurfaced. They had to be old news by now. And he'd not been anywhere near a TV camera in a year and a half except for...

"Aw... You didn't know."

Kellie's concern only put him more on guard, raising the hairs on the back of his neck with a sense of foreboding—

the same prickling precognition he'd used to get out of the battlefield before a sniper attack.

"I thought it was strange, given your aversion to the press when we were together, but I figured you'd gotten over it since you appeared to be working so closely with Dr. Flynn in the clips." Kellie pulled out her phone, tapped on the screen a few times, then handed the device to Jake. "Take a look for yourself."

The footage showed him and Molly after Dr. Dave's party, both of them grinning as she asked him to go on a whale-watching cruise. His universe imploded as her words from that night echoed through his head.

"I'll make sure they edit you out…"

"Are you two involved?" Kellie asked. "I promise not to mention it in my story."

Wendy knocked before sticking her head inside the office, giving Kellie a disparaging glance before focusing on Jake. "Sorry, Doc, but the patient load is backing up out here. Any chance you can give us a hand?"

Oddly numb now, Jake pushed to his feet and walked to the door, his movements robotic and his smile stiff, all his systems working on autopilot as he struggled to process what he'd just learned.

That footage had been leaked and Molly had never said a word. She'd known about his past, known about what he'd dealt with at his commendation and with Kellie, and she'd still allowed those clips to be released without a word to him. She'd promised to have his shots edited out. He'd trusted her, opened up to her, let himself be vulnerable—and look where it had gotten him.

His chest caved, a black hole forming where his heart had been.

Molly had betrayed his trust—just like Kellie had years before.

We need to talk.

Damn right they did.

Jake walked away without another word to his ex and grabbed a chart from the nearest holder. Tonight he'd meet with Molly and demand to know why she'd lied.

Then he'd close his heart to her and what they'd shared. Once and for all.

CHAPTER THIRTEEN

MOLLY MET JAKE in the lobby of her hotel at eight o'clock sharp.

After much soul-searching, and anguished hours of wavering, she'd concluded that telling him about the leaked footage was only fair, given how close they'd become. It was in direct violation of what her network wanted, but she'd deal with that fallout when the time came. What she felt with Jake was much more important.

As he helped Molly into the passenger side of his truck the memories flooded back—his taste, his scent, his touch. His fingers brushed lightly against her skin and she couldn't suppress an answering shiver. They both wore the same outfits they'd worn at Dr. Dave's party, she noticed.

"Where are we going?" Molly asked, nervous energy suffusing her system as Jake climbed into the driver's seat, started the engine, and headed toward downtown Anchorage. She glanced at his strong, tapered fingers on the steering wheel, remembering the feel of those fingers on her body.

"Ursa," he said, not looking at her, his tone terse.

"As in bear?"

"The food's excellent. Modern American cuisine. Three-star Michelin rating."

His voice held a chilled edge, but she brushed it off. He was probably tired. They'd both had long days.

"Bobby seems to be doing okay in his clean room," she said, to fill the silence.

"Hopefully you'll find out what's wrong soon and he won't be there long."

He stared straight ahead, no expression, tension evident

around his mouth and eyes. Brian had worn that same flat look toward the end. The thought did little to quiet her unease.

"Then you can get back to your life in Chicago and I can get back to giving the ER my full attention again."

And there it was. The inevitable end.

Molly's self-doubts resurfaced, intensified, stung like hell—even though he was right. She'd gone into this affair with her eyes open. There couldn't really be anything permanent between them because of the distance factor, no matter how she might wish things were different.

He wouldn't want to offer her forever, knowing she'd be gone soon, and she couldn't offer him more than she already had either. Not with her show's crazy schedule and chaos at the network. Then again, after she told him about the leaked footage he probably wouldn't want to be with her anymore anyway.

Her chest squeezed and she offered him an easy escape route. "We don't have to go out if it's a problem."

"No, no. We definitely need to talk. About a lot of things."

His definitive statement made the knots in her stomach tighten all the more. Gone was the easy banter they'd shared during the whale-watching cruise and later that evening at the pub, gone the connection and closeness that had grown between them after their torrid night in each other's arms. It seemed they were back to chilly courtesy and wary politeness again.

They pulled up to the curb in front of the restaurant a few minutes later. Red-hued neon highlighted the beige stone exterior and surrounded a huge portrait of a snarling bear. Jake handed his keys to the valet, then helped Molly from the truck, though he let her go almost immediately. She missed the guiding comfort of his hand on her lower back.

Inside, the maître d' showed them to a cozy corner table near a crackling fireplace and took their coats. The interior's wood tones were complemented by plush oriental rugs and cool river rock stone walls. Modern paintings from local artists and sparkling crystal chandeliers completed the eclectic chic ambiance.

A waiter appeared with menus and poured them each a goblet of water. "Would you care for something from the bar this evening or an appetizer?"

"Two glasses of Chardonnay. Thanks." Jake sat back and toyed with his silverware, his expression dour. "What did you want to talk to me about?"

Molly took a sip of her water, still unsure how to breach the topic of the leaked footage and doing her best not to revert to the old patterns of withdrawal and defensiveness that she'd learned over years of dealing with her father.

"There've been some changes at the network."

Jake gave a curt nod but remained silent. He waited until the sommelier had finished pouring their wine before continuing, still not meeting her gaze.

"Such as?"

"They're giving my father his own show."

Jake drank his wine, watching her closely over the rim of his glass. "Surprised he's got time, what with running the world and all."

Tell him, Molly chided herself, hating the fact that she wasn't braver.

This was her life, her choice, her mess to clean up. She just wished she could've had one more night in Jake's arms before it was all over.

Grief and loss pinched her heart and she squeezed her eyes closed against the pain. Just do it.

After a deep breath for courage, she sat forward. "There's something I need to tell you. About those times when my crew was filming and you happened to be there."

Jake finally met her eyes, thunderclouds gathering in his gaze. "Yes?"

"Well…" Molly swallowed hard against the lump of

dread in her throat and forced the words out in a tumble of regret. "Somehow the footage you were in ended up all over the Internet before the network edited you out of it. MedStar's attorneys have forbidden me from saying anything, but I wanted to tell you after what happened between us and—"

"Isn't it convenient how that worked?"

That tiny muscle ticked near Jake's clenched jaw again, the same as she remembered from the night of Dr. Dave's party, when he'd been confronting her father. Not a good sign. Not at all.

"How long have you known?"

Molly winced, not even trying to play dumb. What was the point?

Her heart tumbled to somewhere near her toes and any bit of appetite she'd had was gone, replaced now with the bitter taste of remorse. "Two days."

"Two days." Jake leaned back and crossed his arms, his expression hard and hurt. "Two days you've known about this and you didn't tell me."

"I wanted to, but then this whole thing with my father getting his own show blew up, and Bobby took a turn for the worse, and the attorneys didn't want me to say anything, and—"

"I trusted you, Molly."

"I know. And I'm so, so sorry. Please believe me. I wanted to tell you, but I wasn't sure how to say it and I didn't want to lose—"

"Jake!"

A brunette rushed up to their table—the same one Molly remembered from the photo in Jake's house. The beginning of a headache throbbed behind Molly's temples, but it was no match for the pain of betrayal clawing through her heart. Had sleeping with her all been part of Jake getting back with his ex? Was that why Kellie was back in town? Had he been seeing Kellie too, the whole time he'd been wooing Molly?

You have no claim on him, remember? her not-so-helpful rational brain stated. That fact did nothing to relieve the ache of loss in Molly's bones.

"Fancy seeing you again so soon, Jake," Kellie said, her gaze locked on Molly. "Aren't you going to introduce me?"

"Molly, this is Kellie Hughes, my ex-fiancée." Jake stared at the tabletop, his expression hard as granite. "Kellie, this is Dr. Flynn."

Anguish swelled inside her. It seemed Jake had reverted to using her professional title.

Molly knew she had no right to feel upset. She'd broken her promises, betrayed Jake's trust, betrayed the fragile bond that had formed between them. Gone. It was all gone now, and she had no one to blame but herself.

Perhaps Brian was right—her father too. Maybe she was just better off alone. Alone and completely driven by her work. Alone and lonely and safe.

Except safe didn't hold the same appeal it once had.

Torn and twisted inside, Molly extended a shaky hand to Kellie. "Nice to meet you."

"You're Roger Flynn's daughter, aren't you?" Kellie's cat-that-ate-the-canary grin widened. "Jake mentioned it earlier today, when we met in his office. I'm here to interview your father. I'll be traveling up to Fairbanks General tomorrow, actually. But since I'm in Anchorage tonight, I thought perhaps you might have a chance to talk with me too, maybe between breaks in filming your show? News just broke about his new slot in MedStar's fall schedule, right after Diagnosis Critical. Early buzz says it's going to be a big hit. You must be thrilled."

"Thrilled" wasn't the first word Molly would choose. Alarmed, appalled, heartsick—any of those seemed way more apropos. But at the moment she felt as if she was drowning in a big cesspool of recrimination.

Jake stared at her from across the table, his lips tight and his gaze unyielding, most likely detesting her over the leaked footage. Beside him Kellie watched her as if she was some kind of circus oddity—the same look her father's friends had used to give young Molly during her performances at home. As if they could see all her faults, all her foibles, all her flaws. As if they were just waiting for Molly to screw up.

"About the interview," Kellie persisted. "I promise not to take up too much of your time."

"No interview." Molly forced the words past her tight vocal cords. "I'm sorry."

"Too bad." Kellie didn't sound disappointed. "But your father told me to expect as much. He said you were…different. Now, it's obvious what he meant."

Obvious that you're weird. Obvious that you're awkward. Obvious that you're unlovable.

Why had she ever thought this would work with Jake? Seeing him sitting there with his ex, both so beautiful and poised and perfect, she wondered why he would ever choose someone like her for more than just a casual fling.

He wouldn't.

Molly blinked at Jake as Kellie abruptly walked away, eyes stinging at the realization. She wouldn't cry. She wouldn't. But the harder she tried to stop the tears, the more they struggled to escape. It seemed she'd kept her emotions under wraps too long. Now that the floodgates were open there was no closing them.

"Are you crying?" Jake asked, incredulous. "Dammit, Molly—"

She tuned him out. She'd heard all those taunts from her father too many times to count.

"Stop crying. Tears are for weaklings. Your emotions are your enemy."

Molly knew all that—knew her feelings would only cause her trouble—and still she'd taken the gamble, gone with her gut, chosen a glorious night in Jake's arms over a million days of nothingness in her father's harsh, cold world.

Sniffling, Molly searched her handbag for a tissue and found her phone buzzing with a text from Gladys.

Bobby in RD.

"I need to go." Molly stood and tossed her napkin on the table.

"So that's it, then?" Jake rose as well, scowling, his eyes glittering with anger. "You're done? We're not even discussing this? You're just going to walk out and to hell with us?"

"There is no 'us,' Jake. There never was. You know that as well as I do."

Molly rushed to the lobby to get her coat while swiping the back of her hand across her wet cheeks, Jake hot on her heels. If this was what it was like to live with your heart on your sleeve, where it could get broken and trampled, then it was awful.

Molly dialed the hospital, waiting anxiously for Gladys to pick up. At Jake's pointed stare, she said, "Bobby's in respiratory distress."

The words emerged more impassioned than she'd intended, but her heart felt ripped out and stomped on. She'd trusted Jake too. Trusted him enough to let him see the real her, opened her heart and soul to him—which had been a mistake. She'd known better than to let him in, let him see her flaws. Honestly, she should be thankful. Thankful that he'd reminded her of why it was better, safer, to keep to herself.

"But he's in a clean room," Jake said softly, his tanned face growing pale.

"I know that." Molly tugged on her coat before pushing outside to hail a taxi, her irritation at herself for being such a trusting idiot bubbling over into her snarky response. "I'm the one who put him there, remember?"

"How could Bobby go into respiratory distress in a sterile environment?"

"Your guess is as good as mine right now."

A cab swerved up to the curb and Molly opened the door. Her cheeks were burning and her eyes felt puffy, but she had to pull herself together so she could save Bobby.

She climbed into the back seat, saying to the driver, "I need to get to Anchorage Mercy as soon as possible, please."

"Molly, wait!" Jake called from the curb.

"I can't wait, Jake. I'm sorry. Goodbye."

As the car pulled away more tears welled. For the remainder of her time here Molly would have to see Jake as just a work associate—nothing more.

Goodbye fun…goodbye affection. Goodbye love.

Jake stared after the cab, focusing on the red glow of the receding taillights, wondering how in the world this whole thing had ended so horribly. And, yeah, he was fed up. Rightfully so. He was the wronged party. So why did he now feel like as much of a bully as Molly's ass of a father?

Dammit.

He scrubbed a hand over his face and leaned against the side of the cold brick building. Molly had needed him tonight—needed his support tonight against Kellie—but he'd been so wrapped up in his past hurts and bruised ego he'd left her flailing.

Yes, he was upset about the footage. Yes, she should've told him. Yes, he felt betrayed. But as his righteous fury burned away he was left feeling raw and exposed.

Part of him wanted to run after that taxi and make it stop. His past, though, kept him rooted to the spot. After all, he'd allowed himself to trust a woman completely before and look where that had gotten him. Kellie had had excuses, reasons, lies aplenty for why she'd done what she'd done—why she'd left him and run off alone to New York, why she'd never looked back.

Stupid. You're so damned stupid, his brain said. You're

an ER doc. Why would a brilliant, successful woman choose you over the bright lights and big city?

It was embarrassing. Shameful. If he had any brains at all, he'd have learned from his mistakes and moved on from Kellie to make wiser choices in his future relationships. Stay away from women who'd only leave him behind in the dust when something bigger or better came along, when the next huge case beckoned.

Why not you? his heart asked. Molly's not Kellie.

And she wasn't. He knew that. They were as different as night and day. Kellie only cared about herself. Molly was selfless and kind and giving. They were different.

Are they? Brain again. Always the cynic.

His mixed reactions made his gut twist.

Still torn, he lingered outside, battling the urge to call Molly and tell her that he loved her, that he would do anything to erase his knee-jerk reaction to the news about the leaked footage and the unexpected and unwelcome arrival of Kellie at their table and beg her forgiveness, but he couldn't.

He couldn't change what he'd done because he didn't want to hurt her. Couldn't promise her something he couldn't deliver. Truth was, once Bobby's case was over she'd be gone and he'd be left to deal with the aftermath alone, as always.

No. They'd both gone into this knowing it was temporary, fleeting.

Still, that was no reason to hurt her the way he had in the restaurant. No reason to lash out and strike all those vulnerable areas of hers just because he knew which buttons to push, same as she did with him.

God, what a mess.

Too late, Jake realized the anger and betrayal he'd felt inside the restaurant had been directed more at past wrongs with Kellie than it had been toward the woman who'd just left for the hospital.

Each time he closed his eyes all Jake could see was Molly's tearstained face, the way she'd shrunk in on herself as Kellie had repeated her father's insults.

Different. Like that was a bad thing. To Jake, "different" sounded pretty damned wonderful.

You're such a jerk.

At least on that point his heart and his brain were united in their sentiment.

Distracted, Jake stalked back into the restaurant and hailed their waiter. Bobby was in trouble and Molly needed him and that was all that mattered.

Ignoring the curious stares of the other patrons, he tossed a fifty-dollar bill on the table to cover their drinks and un-eaten appetizer.

"Wait, sweetie." Kellie laid a hand on his forearm as he tried to leave. "I was hoping to talk more—especially since your friend is gone."

"Molly is not my friend." Jake pulled free, then rushed back toward the exit. "She's the most brilliant and exasperating woman I've ever known. And I am not your sweetie. Not anymore."

Kellie kept pace beside him, her gaze narrowed. "You love her, don't you?"

"What? No." Yes. He moved outside and handed his ticket to the valet. "I need to get to the hospital. Go back to Roger Flynn, Kellie. We have nothing left to talk about."

"But—" Kellie said as his truck swerved up to the curb.

"No. Don't." Jake tipped the valet, then started around the front of his vehicle. "I'm over it. Over what happened. Move on, Kellie. Good luck with your career in New York."

"If you think that woman will give up her life and her show for you, you're wrong," Kellie said, lifting her chin. "She's more like her father than you think. He told me so."

"Molly is nothing like her father. And you of all people shouldn't believe everything you hear." Jake yanked open the driver's side door. "Now, if you'll excuse me, I've got my best friend's life to save. Safe travels."

CHAPTER FOURTEEN

HOURS LATER, MOLLY sat in the small office-slash-observation area attached to Bobby's clean room, going over her patient's chart for what seemed like the billionth time and trying not to think about what had happened with Jake.

Bobby's condition had deteriorated rapidly—so much so that they'd put him on a ventilator and into a medically induced coma to give his poor lungs a chance to recuperate.

The staff had finished re-sterilizing the entire clean room again, screening for all outside contaminates—including testing the rubber gloves and the latex tubing of his IVs. He had no piercings, no implants, no metal pins in his body of any kind. Even the sterile solution flowing into his veins to keep him hydrated had been analyzed for allergens. Nothing had been found.

It didn't make sense.

Molly took a deep breath and stared at the documentation. The only other possible source of the inflammation was an autoimmune disorder, but they'd already screened for those too—multiple times—and the tests had all been negative, as had his bloodwork.

Meaning they were right back where they'd started.

Speaking of right back where you started…

Ugh. Molly's mind filled with images of Jake's angry expression, his ice-cold stare, the way he'd sat there while his ex-fiancée had spewed her father's hurtful words and done nothing.

Logic said being this upset about Jake not caring for her was silly. One whale-watching cruise followed by a night of mind-blowing passion did not a true relationship make. No matter how badly she might have wished it were otherwise.

But her beloved facts and analysis were of little comfort tonight.

Groaning, Molly put her head down on her arms atop the small desk. More tears stung her eyes, though she refused to let them fall. She'd gone from one extreme to the other during her time here, and in the process had blown any chance of a future between her and Jake.

Molly pulled a tissue from the box beside her as moments of their time together flickered across her mind like a sappy movie—the whale-watching cruise, their first kiss in the workout room, the evening at the pub when Jake had all but dragged her home to make love with her.

Gone. Those things were all gone and she was back in her lonely hospital fortress with only the monotonous whoosh and puff of Bobby's ventilator to keep her company.

Frustrated, Molly tipped her head back and rubbed her eyes.

Bobby's case. That was what she needed to concentrate on now—not her disastrous love life.

Think, Flynn. Think.

The next step was to do one last full-body CT scan. Go over the films inch by inch to see if they revealed anything previously missed. That would also keep her busy for a while, and stop her from obsessing over her monumental screwup with the man she loved.

She reached for the phone to call Scheduling, then halted. A voice echoed around her—deep, rich, tinged with sadness.

"Hey."

Jake.

Molly looked around quickly to see where he was, but she was alone. Then she glanced at the small speaker for the PA system nestled into the wall beside the desk. He was talking to Bobby next door. She rose slightly to peer over the sill of the glass window separating the two rooms.

Jake stood near Bobby's bedside, dressed in a head-to-

toe white hazmat suit. Only the upper third of his face was visible through the clear plastic shield in the hood, but the regret in his gaze was evident as he took Bobby's limp hand in his gloved one.

"I'm so sorry, bud. After all those missions in Kandahar this was never how it was supposed to end. Never. Thank you for saving my life, for shielding me when that IED went off. With all those Taliban creeping through every crack and alleyway and rooftop, armed to the teeth, there's no way I would've made it if you hadn't been there…"

His words cracked and his brave façade crumbled.

"I'd be dead. If it wasn't for you I wouldn't be here today, and for that I owe you more than I can ever repay. You don't like me to bring it up, but you are and always will be a true hero."

Molly sat back, new memories flooding her mind about the case—Bobby's comment to Jake about thinking he had to watch over him. Bobby's hallucinations about people in the walls and ceiling.

"Thank you for saving my life, for shielding me when that IED went off…"

Improvised Explosive Devices were constructed by terrorist cells and made of cheap materials—metal canisters filled with nuts and bolts or ball bearings, packed tight with explosives. She reexamined Bobby's initial history and physical, taken in the ER.

Activity engaged in prior to dermatitis—polishing team trophies.

Nuts, bolts, ball bearings, trophies—they all had one thing in common.

Metal.

She grabbed the phone on the wall. "Radiology? This is Dr. Flynn. I need to schedule Bobby Templeton for a full-body CT scan."

After giving the technician her patient's information,

Molly rushed out into the hallway and nearly ran over Jake, who was removing his hazmat suit.

"I know what's wrong with Bobby."

He froze, eyes wide. "What?"

"A metal allergy. I've got him scheduled for a full-body scan in half an hour."

"But they've already done multiple scans and found nothing." Jake frowned, tossing the disposable suit in a nearby biohazard bin. "Why would something show up this time?"

"Because this time I know what I'm looking for."

Molly's words rushed out in a jumble of excitement, her heart pounding with the thrill of discovery and the fact that Jake wasn't glaring at her with cool contempt anymore.

"Where was Bobby positioned during the IED explosion?"

Jake's gaze narrowed. "You were eavesdropping?"

Guilt prickled Molly's cheeks. She stared at the center of his chest because she couldn't meet his gaze, knowing how he felt—or didn't feel—about her. It would hurt more than she could stand.

"I'm sorry I violated your trust. I'm sorry about the leaked footage and about overhearing your private conversation with Bobby. I'm sorry for everything—more than you'll ever know. But if I'm right we can save your best friend's life."

"Molly, I…"

Jake moved closer—close enough for her to catch his warm, comforting scent, mixed with the Betadine he'd used to scrub down with earlier, and her knees wanted to buckle from the weight of what she'd lost with him. He lifted his hand as if to caress her cheek, then let it fall to his side as he stepped back again, his expression unreadable.

"One more scan. But if you don't find anything it's over. Bobby lives out his last hours in peace."

Molly gave a small nod. "I'll do everything in my power to save him. I promise."

"Right flank."

"Sorry?" She frowned, meeting his gaze as the elevator doors dinged open.

"You asked what position Bobby was in when the IED exploded. He was leaning over me, with his back to the bomb. Since he was wearing Kevlar armor on his upper body, I'd say your best bet to find something would be in the right flank area."

Four hours later Jake sat in his office, staring at the same patient file he'd had open since he'd walked in. He'd long ago finished his documentation, and things in the ER had never been slower. The quiet was enough to drive him bonkers. He'd considered going upstairs to Radiology, to see what Molly had found, but given the current strain between them he'd probably only end up saying or doing something else he regretted.

And when it came to Molly…boy, did he regret.

He regretted reacting like an ass when she'd finally told him about the leaked footage. Regretted sitting there while Kellie repeated Roger Flynn's vile insults, knowing how awfully Molly's family had treated her for her differences. Regretted not rushing to Molly's defense and begging her forgiveness.

Sighing, he rubbed his tired eyes and slumped in his chair, too exhausted to stop images from the past few weeks from flooding his brain. Molly standing up to him at that accident scene. Her surprisingly strong punches in the workout room. Their first kiss…

God, that kiss.

She was all heat and light and sweetness—the way she'd cajoled him out of his depression after that gunshot victim passed away. The way she'd given herself so beautifully to him when they'd made love…

He didn't deserve her. Probably never had.

Worst of all, Jake had known what they had was fleeting,

and he should have treasured it even more because of it. Instead he'd thrown it all away, because he was too damned scared of trusting and getting his heart shattered again.

And in the end, that was exactly what had happened anyway.

Cursing his own stupidity, Jake switched on his computer to check his emails.

His web browser loaded. To one side of the screen was a scrolling list of top news stories—the state of the economy, the latest forest fires in California, some celebrity's mega-million-dollar birthday bash in Dubai.

Near the bottom of the feed, one headline caught his eye: Sparks fly between reality TV doc and ex–war hero over star hockey player's treatment.

Curiosity got the better of him and Jake clicked on the link. It took him to one of those tabloid websites that wrote the most salacious articles possible. This one suggested that there was more to his and Molly's working relationship than medicine. Not a lie, but not their business either.

He scrolled farther down the page. The article went on to question Bobby's notorious dating past and his puck-bunny groupies. Near the bottom were several screen shots—Jake and Molly outside Bobby's room, staring each other down like a Mexican stand-off, both of them caring for Bobby during his seizure, both of them after Dr. Dave's dinner party, discovering the yohimbe tea.

His heart ached and his chest squeezed—and that was when he knew the truth. The truth was he'd fallen hard for Molly Flynn, despite all the reasons why he shouldn't. Despite all his well-crafted barriers and walls. She'd crushed them all with just a smile, an awkward ramble, a kiss.

His phone rang and Jake answered, distracted. "Ryder."

"We found it," Molly said, her tone triumphant.

"What? Where?"

"A bolt, about one point four millimeters, near his right iliac crest. Tiny, and deeply embedded in scar tissue. Easily missed. I'd like to schedule Bobby for surgery as soon as we get him stabilized."

"Uh…yes. Yes!"

Jake squeezed his eyes shut, trying to take it all in. Bobby would be okay. His vow was fulfilled, his debt repaid—all thanks to Molly. "Have them call Dr. Minor. He's the best ortho guy in Anchorage."

"Okay. Bobby's going to be fine!"

Molly's optimism had bolstered Jake's listless spirits. He wanted to reach through the phone line and hug her tight. He wanted to kiss her silly. He wanted to drop to his knees and beg her to take him back.

Instead, he managed a gruff, "Have the staff call me once he's in Recovery."

"Of course."

Jake stood there for several seconds after the call ended. Bobby would be okay. Bobby would be okay, and Molly would leave, and life would get back to normal.

He should be happy. "Normal" was what he'd worked so hard to achieve.

So why, then, did normal suddenly seem like the most awful thing in the world?

CHAPTER FIFTEEN

"SURPRISE!" A GAGGLE of enormous hockey players bar-reled into Bobby Templeton's room, some carrying bal-loons or gifts, all wearing the Anoraks's trademark yellow and black jerseys.

Molly and her crew stepped aside. They'd just wrapped the final shots for the episode and Neal wanted to get some last candid footage of her patient making a full recovery.

It had been a week since the surgery to remove the bolt, and Bobby's condition had improved dramatically. So much so that he could be released in a day or two.

One of Bobby's teammates—a huge man with a shaggy black beard and a gold tooth—leaned over and gave Bobby a bear hug, slapping him so hard on the shoulder it made Molly wince.

"Dude! You had me worried."

"Me too," Bobby said, accepting another bruising hug from yet another teammate. "You guys won't believe the sh—" He glanced over at Rob and his camera. "The stuff they did to me. Put me in isolation, probed me, gave me enough isotopes to make me radioactive."

"Whoa!" the team said collectively.

"I know, right?" Bobby said, clearly loving the spotlight. "It was so bad."

He looked over at Molly and winked, and she couldn't hide a smile.

"Do you need anything?" the team's coach asked his most valuable player.

"Nah." Bobby pushed himself up straighter in the bed. "I'll be better once I get out of here and back home again."

Back home. The words were bittersweet for Molly. Usually at the end of a case she couldn't wait to get back to Chicago, but not this time. There was no one waiting for her and nothing but chaos at the network.

At least she'd come to find some clarity about her situation. In the wee hours of the morning, unable to sleep, Molly had taken a hard look at her life. She'd begun Diagnosis Critical because she'd wanted to make a name for herself outside the glare of her father's spotlight, to escape his bullying and prove she was strong and capable. She'd done all those things and it was time to move on. She'd had enough.

As the sun had risen over the snowcapped Chugach mountains Molly had realized something else too. She'd come here to cure Bobby, but she'd ended up curing herself. It was time to stand up to her bully of a father and put an end to his control over her life. She was who she was and it was time to stop apologizing for it and start embracing it.

Here in Anchorage, for the first time, she'd found people who respected her, patients who needed her, and the most gorgeous scenery she'd ever beheld. But, more than anything, she'd found Jake. He'd taught her to embrace her differences, to open up and experience things she'd only ever dreamed of prior to this trip.

For that, and for so many other reasons, she loved him. Even if he would never feel the same or forgive her for breaking his trust.

She glanced over and saw him leaning against the doorframe of Bobby's room, his gaze guarded. He hiked his chin toward her and gestured at the hall.

"Be right back," she said to Rob.

"Go get 'em, Mol." Her cameraman grinned.

Molly followed Jake down to the door of the meditation chapel, attempting to fill the awkward silence by stating the obvious. "Bobby's doing well."

"Yeah," Jake said, facing her once they were alone in the hall. "About what happened—"

"It's fine."

"It's not fine." Jake watched her from across the span of a few feet, but it might as well have been a few miles, given the distance between them emotionally. "I owe you an apology."

"No, you don't. You had every right to be furious about that footage. And the things Kellie repeated from my father weren't anything I haven't heard before."

By tonight Molly would be on a flight home to Chicago. Anchorage would be nothing but a dot on a map. And this man she loved with all her heart would move on with his life and she'd move on with hers.

The words hurt, but Molly forced them out anyway. "You trusted me and I betrayed that trust. And I'm so, so sorry." Blinking hard, she took a step away. "Now, if you'll excuse me, I have some paperwork to finish."

"Wait." Jake handed her an oblong white object. "Here."

"What's this?" Molly frowned. "Is that a smiley face?"

"It's an Inupiat piece—a carved walrus tooth."

"Oh." She held the precious treasure, still warm from his body. "I can't take this, Jake. I'm sure it means a lot to you."

"It does." He reached out and tucked a stray lock of hair behind her ear. "You do too."

Molly tried her hardest, but nothing would hold back the tears. "Jake—"

"C'mon. I want to show you something."

He ushered her into the chapel, where Neal was setting up one of the monitors they used in the production room. Jake guided Molly into a seat before the screen then took the chair beside her.

"I can't go any longer without telling you I'm sorry too. Sorry for overreacting and sorry for not standing up for you at the restaurant. You've changed since coming to Anchorage Mercy, Molly. But I've changed too. Because of you."

Sniffling, Molly chuckled. "Yeah, I've changed into a blubbering wreck."

"No, you've discovered the loving, caring woman lurking inside you." He cupped her face, his thumb stroking her cheek gently. "I always knew she was in there, waiting to emerge."

Her heart pinched at his sweet words and more tears flowed. "The problem is, since I've started crying I don't know how to stop it."

"I've got an idea how to fix that, Bolt."

Jake leaned in to kiss her. Before their lips could meet, however, a quick knock sounded on the door, followed by Dr. Dave and Rob shouldering their way inside.

"Ah, Molly!" Dr. Dave said, his jolly blue gaze darting between her and Jake. "Gladys said I might find you in here. I'm not interrupting anything, am I?"

Squeezing Jake's hand, Molly shook her head. "No, no. Please have a seat."

"What I'm about to say may come as a surprise," Dr. Dave said. "But Anchorage Mercy is starting a new Diagnostic Medicine program soon and I'd like to put in your name for the chief director position."

Molly looked from Dr. Dave to Jake, then back again. She hadn't given much thought to the next step in her career. Hadn't even mentioned to her crew that she was leaving the network.

"Wow. I'm flattered."

"What about your show?" Jake asked.

"Yeah, what about the show?" Rob and Neal stood beside the small group. "Something you'd like to tell us, Mol?"

She cringed. "Sorry, guys, but I decided last night that Bobby's case is going to be my last episode of Diagnosis Critical. I've been wavering about signing on for another season and…" she snuggled closer to Jake and smiled "…I've decided not to renew."

"Aw…" Rob and Neal hugged her, then each other. "Congrats, you two."

"Being here in Alaska has helped me realize a lot of things—not the least of which is that I need to get a life."

Molly smiled. "One of my own choosing this time—not one based on what anyone else thinks I should want or to prove myself to someone."

"Right. Well, then…" Dr. Dave headed for the door. "Please give my offer careful consideration, Dr. Flynn. I think Anchorage Mercy would be a great fit for your skills."

"I'll give you an answer by the end of next week, Dr. Dave. Thank you."

"Have a safe journey home," Dr. Dave said on his way out.

Except Anchorage felt way more like home than Chicago ever had.

In a rare burst of spontaneity, Molly rushed over and yanked open the chapel door, calling into the hall after Dr. Dave. "Forget waiting. Yes. I want the job. Put my name in, please."

"Marvelous! I'll call the board this afternoon and let them know," he said from near the elevators. "You can stay with Sara and me until you get settled here. No worries."

"Thanks again for everything, Dr. Dave."

Molly stepped back into the chapel, where Jake and her crew waited.

"Well, I guess that's it, then…"

"I'm glad you're sticking around, Bolt." Jake came up to her, slipping his arm around her shoulders and pulling Molly closer. "But you have other living options too."

"I do?"

"Yeah." He flashed that sexy half-smile that made her knees go all tingly. "You can move in with me, if you want."

A fresh wave of tears flooded her eyes and she didn't even try to stop them this time. "Yes, I want," she said, grinning through her sniffles. "I want to so much it hurts."

"Good." He kissed her quickly. "Then we've got lots of plans to make, Bolt. But first there's something you need to see."

"Dr. Ryder taped a special ending for the episode and we

thought you might like to watch it before it airs in a couple of months," Neal said.

"Really?" Molly gave Jake a disbelieving look. "I thought you hated being on camera."

"I do." He cuddled her tight to his side again. "But I'm willing to make sacrifices when it comes to you, Bolt."

"We ready to roll?" Rob asked, holding the remote for the flat screen. "Neal and I have a flight to catch tonight."

"Let's do it," Molly said.

The screen flickered and Jake appeared, tapping a little microphone pinned to his scrubs. "Is this on?"

"We're ready," Neal prompted on screen. "Can you state your name?"

"Dr. Jake Ryder."

"And what's your position at Anchorage Mercy?"

"I'm the Head of Emergency Medicine."

"Tell us how it was, working with Dr. Molly Flynn."

"At first it was…tricky. At least for me. But we became a great team."

"Do you believe in her unorthodox treatment protocols?"

"No, not always. But I do believe in her. She's the most brilliant physician I've ever met. Molly has a huge heart and a wonderful capacity to see what others can't. She's truly special." Onscreen, Jake's voice roughened with emotion. "I feel honored to know her and I'm so grateful for all she's done here."

"Okay, Dr. Ryder. Anything else you'd like to say?"

"Yes." Jake looked directly into the camera. "The local Inupiat tribes have a saying: We are forever remembered by the tracks we leave. Molly, your footprints will always stay on the hearts of everyone here at Anchorage Mercy. Especially mine."

The screen went black once more.

"Oh, Jake," Molly said through more tears. "I love you."

"I love you too, Bolt." He meant the words with every fiber of his being.

Rob started packing away the gear, grinning from ear to ear. "Just make sure we get invited back for the wedding, okay?"

Jake snorted. "Like we'd get married without the crew that brought us together!"

"I thought Bobby brought us together," Molly said, frowning.

"Him too, Bolt." Jake laughed, then pulled his phone from the waistband of his scrubs. "Oops. I need to get back to the ER. Looks like we're getting slammed again."

"Want any help?" She pushed to her feet beside him.

"Sure." Jake took Molly's hand and headed for the door, asking the guys, "When's your flight?"

"Ten thirty tonight," Neal said. "When are you flying back, Mol?"

"I got my flight changed to tomorrow morning."

Jake's heart stumbled. That meant they could have one more night together.

They waved to the guys, then headed to his ER. Jake grabbed the first chart from the queue and perused the history and physical before handing the file to Molly.

"Oh, Bolt. You'll love this one."

"Why? Is it difficult?" she asked, frowning at the notes.

"No. Just the cutest couple ever."

"I thought that was us?"

"You're right. It is us."

He bent to give Molly a quick kiss, then noticed Wendy watching them. She gave Jake two thumbs-up before rushing off to assist one of the residents.

"Ready?"

"Ready," Molly said, and they walked into Trauma Bay Three together.

CHAPTER SIXTEEN

Eight weeks later...

"Do I look okay, Bolt?" Jake asked Molly as they stood in the grand foyer of the Drake Hotel in downtown Chicago.

Honestly, Molly wanted nothing more than to whisk him off to a room upstairs, strip off his tailor-made suit, toss him on the bed and make love to him until they were both senseless with ecstasy. But first they had to face Martha's dreaded baby shower extraordinaire.

And Molly's father.

Leaving Jake behind in Anchorage had been the hardest thing Molly had ever done, but she'd had things to settle here in Chicago. She'd resigned from the network, sublet her tiny apartment on Lake Shore Drive, gotten all her things packed and had a proper send-off with Rob and Neal.

All that was left were her farewells to her family.

Those would come today.

Later tonight she and Jake were flying back to Alaska on the red-eye to start a new chapter together. Dr. Dave had pushed through the hospital board's vote and secured her the job of Head of Diagnostic Medicine at Anchorage Mercy, so Molly had been busy telecommuting—signing contracts and hiring staff—and she couldn't wait to assume her new post and start seeing patients in the new facilities the hospital had revamped for her department.

It was like a dream come true. All thanks to the support of the man beside her.

"You look devastatingly handsome," Molly said, smoothing Jake's tie and giving him a quick kiss.

Then, hand in hand, they walked into the hotel's French Room.

Molly had done her best with the decorations, given her limited time and her mother's constant nitpicking, but as she saw the place now she thought the pretty silver and gold streamers complemented the elegant room's pastel green silk wall coverings and the swirling indigo patterns in the custom carpets.

Above, crystal basket chandeliers shimmered, and deep blue satin damask draperies covered the windows overlooking Lake Michigan in the distance. Over a hundred of her parents' colleagues and Martha's friends milled about in the space, chatting or snacking on obscenely expensive lobster and caviar hors d'oeuvres.

"Wow," Jake whispered. "This is quite a spread."

Molly snorted. "Only the best for the Flynns."

"It's about time you two got here." Her mother rushed over.

"Traffic," Molly said, though the real reason for their tardiness was the fact that neither she nor Jake had wanted to leave the cozy little love nest they'd made in their hotel room at the Ritz Carlton on Lakeshore Drive.

"I still don't understand why the two of you didn't stay here at the Drake with the rest of us," Phyllis Flynn said, looking around. "Though you did a decent job on the decorations."

"Thanks. The shower hasn't been my top priority."

Her father joined them, tumbler of whiskey in hand. "Daughter of mine, it's not too late to renegotiate with the network. Though you'll have to take a subpar slot. They've given me your old one."

Molly took a deep breath to relax her tense muscles. "I won't be returning to the network. We discussed this. I've got a new department to run in Anchorage."

"Your loss." Roger Flynn gulped down his drink. "Such a

waste—stuck out there in some hospital on the prairie." He narrowed his icy green gaze on Jake. "I blame you for this."

Jake squeezed Molly's hand. "I gladly take full responsibility, sir."

"No. This was my decision. No one else's." Molly squared her shoulders and raised her chin. "You made my childhood a living hell—but that's over. Starting today, you don't matter anymore. I've got a new life, and a man who loves me just the way I am. I don't need you or your bullying, or your opinions about my life. Not that I ever did."

Roger Flynn shook his head, his expression brimming with disapproval. "Love makes people idiots."

"You're wrong," Molly said, an edge of steel in her tone. "Love makes people human. And unconditional love makes them exceptional. Perhaps if you'd loved me without conditions our relationship wouldn't be what it is today."

"Don't be ridiculous." Her father's scowl darkened. "Why do you think I pushed you so hard all those years? I did it because I loved you—because I saw your enormous potential and wanted you to become all you could be."

"What a crock of—" Jake started.

"I've got this." Molly stopped him, turning back to her father. "The only thing you love is Roger Flynn. You constantly nag and push and force everyone around you to breaking point—and if they snap then you call them weak. I'm sorry you consider me such a disappointment, but I'm through trying to live up to your ideals. This is my life, and I plan to do what makes me happy and fulfilled. That includes running my own department and spending the rest of my days with the man I love. And if you or anyone else can't accept that, please keep it to yourself, okay?"

Her mother huffed. "It isn't polite to raise your voice at a party, dear."

"Maybe not, but it's not polite to make other people feel small either," Molly said, staring at her father in a silent battle of wills.

She'd spent her whole life trying to please this man, trying to earn his love and respect. She'd be damned if she'd back down now.

Roger Flynn finally looked away, hailing a passing waiter for another whiskey. "Well, at least you'll be bringing some much-needed expertise to that wild frontier."

Not quite an apology, but Molly would take it. "I'm looking forward to introducing your theories on halting viral disease progression through enzyme inhibition."

Her father watched Molly over the rim of his glass. "Make sure you give me credit."

"Of course." Molly gave a curt nod and took Jake's hand again.

"Sis!" Martha waddled over, her gait more ungainly as she neared her due date. She was still dressed to the nines in designer maternity wear, with her doting investment banker husband hanging off her arm. "I was hoping you'd be the baby's godmother."

Molly was a bit shocked. "I'd be honored…"

"Good luck in Alaska." Roger Flynn walked away before anyone could respond.

"Call me once you get to Anchorage, dear, to let me know you're safe." Her mother gave Molly a quick air-kiss before bustling off to mingle.

"Can I speak to you outside?"

Jake made their excuses to the expectant parents, then led Molly out into the opulent marble foyer of the hotel. Several paparazzi milled about, looking to snap photos of the many local celebrities attending the party.

Jake pulled Molly into a private little alcove, discreetly covered by plush blue velvet drapes. Her pulse raced. Things had been so magical tonight. Maybe too magical.

But adrenaline still pumped through her system from facing down her father at last, and Molly was riding high on a surge of success. "I can't believe I did that! Did you see his face? I stood up for myself. Me! I did it!"

"Yep, you did, Bolt."

Jake smiled—the lopsided smile that always made her knees go wobbly.

"And I'm so proud of you. I've always respected your amazing abilities as a physician, even if we have differing opinions on some of your treatment choices. But, wow. What you did in there—standing up to that man, that bully, like that. Sweetheart, today my admiration for you and your wonderful heart surpasses everything else. You're incredible, Molly Flynn. Simply incredible."

Despite his impassioned words she didn't miss the flicker of uncertainty in his stormy gray eyes, and a tiny tad of her old insecurity seeped in before she could stop it, dampening her joy.

"What's wrong?" she asked.

"Nothing's wrong." Jake's normally graceful moves turned awkward as he fumbled in his suit pocket and frowned. "I just…"

"Oh, Lord."

Molly's stomach knotted. This might be Brian all over again. She'd finally stood up for herself with one man, but had her newfound gumption cost her the other? Life as the scared, insecure woman who'd hidden inside her sterile, controlled, unemotional world wasn't possible anymore. She couldn't do that again—not even for Jake. But she'd do everything in her power to make things work with him if he gave her the chance.

"Please tell me you're not going to break up with me. I know I've changed since you met me, and things are different with me now than when we first met, but—"

"What? No. I love everything about you, Molly. Never doubt that. It's just that I've got something for you."

Jake went down on one knee, a blue Tiffany box in one hand. Inside was an adorable penguin brooch, with sparkling onyx eyes and black lacquer wings.

"Oh! Wow!" Her smile trembled with surprise. "It's very…cute."

"I spent all day yesterday picking it out while you were wrapping up loose ends at the network. Penguins are kind of our symbol, right? That day in my kitchen you blurted out all those facts about penguins and how they mated for life. I know they're not indigenous to Alaska, but then lots of people are transplants there. Just look at you."

"No. I mean, yes. It's great." Molly stroked her fingers over the pin, her chest squeezing with tenderness and her eyes stinging with unshed tears. She sniffled. "I love it. Really."

"But you were expecting something else?" Jake narrowed his gaze knowingly.

"What?"

She shook her head as he reached into his pocket again. If life had taught her anything, it was that having expectations—especially of the unrealistic kind—was foolish.

She hugged the little penguin to her chest as tears spilled down her cheeks. "No, no. I love it, Jake. Really. And I love you too."

"Good," Jake said, his smile widening.

This time he pulled out a smaller black velvet box and flipped it open with his thumb. Inside sparkled the most beautiful emerald-cut diamond engagement ring Molly had ever seen. She reached out, shaking, to trace her fingertips over the radiant gem, joyful laughter bubbling and fizzing inside her like champagne.

"Molly Flynn, I love you. Will you marry me and be my forever mate?"

Too much. This man was too much. He was all she'd ever wanted and more than she deserved. Overcome with happiness, she felt some of those old random facts gurgling for escape inside her whirling mind. Molly didn't even try to stop them this time. Jake loved her—really, really loved her—quirks and all. She'd take it—and him—forever and ever. Amen.

Molly swiped away her tears with the back of her hand and blinked down at the dear face of the man she loved, reciting statistics like love poems. "People who marry between the ages of twenty-eight and thirty-two have the fewest divorces."

Jake cocked his head, his expression confused. "Is that a yes, Bolt?"

"Yes!" Giddiness rose inside Molly as she knelt too, cupping his cheeks in her trembling hands. "Yes! I love you too and I'd be honored to be your wife."

"Perfect."

Jake slid the ring on her finger, then pulled her in for a deep kiss.

They didn't separate for a long while afterward. At last Jake pulled away, dusting kisses along her cheek to her ear and whispering, "I'm not perfect and I don't profess to be, Molly, but when I'm with you I want to be better. I want to be the man of your dreams."

She rested her forehead against his and smiled, her heart so full it felt as if it might burst forth like a bird from a cage. "You already are, Jake. You already are."

This time when he kissed her she couldn't wait to get back to their love nest at the Ritz Carlton and celebrate their new engagement properly. There'd be plenty of time to tell their friends and family later. Tonight's celebration was for them alone.

A ruckus sounded on the other side of the blue curtains. Jake peered around the edge before giving Molly's hand a reassuring squeeze and helping her to her feet.

"Looks like another local celebrity is arriving for your sister's party," he said. "This is it, Bolt. If we sneak out now there's a chance we won't cause another Internet sensation."

Molly nodded and held on to him tight, ready for her new life to begin. "Let's do it. I'll follow you anywhere, Jake."

"Yeah?" He leaned back for one last, brief kiss over his shoulder.

Molly smiled as they darted out of the alcove, hand in hand, together. "Oh, yeah."

* * * * *

COMING SOON!

We really hope you enjoyed reading this book. If you're looking for more romance, be sure to head to the shops when new books are available on

Thursday
23rd August

MILLS & BOON

Coming next month

THE NURSE'S PREGNANCY MIRACLE
Ann McIntosh

Nychelle tried with all her might to say they shouldn't go any further, but couldn't get the words out. Knowing she needed to tell him the rest of her story battled with the desire making her head swim and her body tingle and thrum with desire.

'Tell me you don't want me,' he said again, and she knew she couldn't. To do so would be to lie.

'I can't. You know I can't. But...'

He didn't wait to hear the rest, just took her mouth in a kiss that made what she'd planned to say fly right out of her brain.

Desire flared, hotter than the Florida sun, and Nychelle surrendered to it, unable and unwilling to risk missing this chance to know David intimately, even if it were just this once. Was it right? Wrong? She couldn't decide — didn't want to try to.

There were so many more things she should explain to him, but she knew she wouldn't. Telling him about the baby when she knew he didn't want a family would destroy whatever it was growing between them. It was craven, perhaps even despicable not to be honest with him, and she hated herself for being underhand, but her mind, heart and body were at war, and she'd already accepted which would win.

She'd deal with the fallout, whatever it might be, tomorrow. Today—this evening—she was going to have what she wanted, live the way she wanted. Enjoy David for this one time. There would only be regrets if she didn't.

His lips were still on hers, demanding, delicious. She'd relived the kisses they'd shared over and over in her mind, but now she realized memory was only a faded facsimile of reality. The touch and taste and scent of him encompassed her, overtaking her system on every level.

Her desperate hands found their way beneath his shirt, and his groan of pleasure was as heartfelt as her joy at the first sensation of his bare skin beneath her palms. His hands, in turn, explored her yearning flesh, stroking her face, then her neck. When they brushed along her shoulders, easing the straps of her sundress away, Nychelle arched against him.

Suddenly it was as though they had both lost all restraint. Arms tight around each other, their bodies moved in concert, their fiercely demanding kisses whipping the flames of arousal to an inferno.

Continue reading
THE NURSE'S PREGNANCY MIRACLE
Ann McIntosh

Available next month
www.millsandboon.co.uk

LET'S TALK
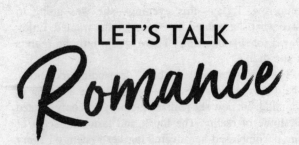
Romance

For exclusive extracts, competitions
and special offers, find us online: